First published in 2020.

Printed in the United States of America.

ISBN 978-1-7348792-1-6

www.vhairijanemoir.com

Illustrations by Eugene Karpenko.

Additional illustrative work by Veronika Gonchar.

Cover design by Yerai Ibarria (illustrated in part by Eugene Karpenko).

For Innes.

Hamish Montgomery and THE CURSED CLAYMORE

VHAIRI JANE MOIR

CONTENTS

1.

A Boy Called Hamish

Hamish Montgomery was one of many. He came from a long, long, looooooooong line of Montgomerys. Eight-hundred and seventy-four years of them to be precise.

Rather than be at the tail-end of such a vast history, Hamish wished he had been alive in those early years, when he imagined there was more going on. Like battles and sword fights.

That stuff didn't happen anymore, sadly, and life at the castle was boring as much as it was lonely for the 10-year-old boy.

"Castle life is the WORST," he would say quietly and not so quietly on a daily basis.

Being a Montgomery meant Hamish's details were recorded in the Drumtipperty Castle family archive along with the rest of his ancestors. Written in curled black ink, his name sat below his father's, Laird Alistair Montgomery, who sat below his father and mother, who sat below his father's grandparents and so on. A complex web of names and pictures spanned the pages, tracking every single Montgomery known to have lived.

Passed down through the ages from generation to generation, the book was bound by a faded red velvet cover with brass corners that were now weathered and dull. A gold badge on the front displayed the family crest – a bird wrapped around a sword. Or at least it once did. Scuffed beyond recognition, the image on the shield was obscure and the breed of bird unknown. Perhaps an eagle. Possibly a hawk. Something of great power and strength. That was the assumption anyway.

Inside the book, the paper had yellowed with age and made a sort of crackling sound when touched, like dry leaves underfoot. On each page, there were names, important dates, and a drawing of each of the castle's occupants, past and present. Hamish, who had no brothers or sisters of his own, insisted his portrait should include his dog, Gorse.

"I won't do it otherwise," he had warned the artist, who came to draw him on his tenth birthday. After all, Gorse was a resident of Drumtipperty too, and his closest, and indeed only, companion.

It was apparent from this old family book that Hamish didn't look much like a Montgomery.

Montgomerys were very tall with reddish-tinged brown hair and blue-grey eyes. Hamish had a mop of sandy blonde hair with dark, almond-shaped eyes, a bit like a deer. He was small for his age but with long, strong arms; he was both an excellent tree climber and ball thrower.

Gorse was also unlike a Montgomery, mostly because he was a dog. A very tall dog, but a dog nonetheless.

Together, the brown-eyed boy and deerhound (Gorse sat several inches taller) were the latest entry in this ancient family record, which meant that like many of Hamish's ancestors on the pages before him, Drumtipperty Castle would one day be his.

Now, Drumtipperty wasn't especially large nor was it grand, not like the castles in books or films with lots of turrets – there was only one, which was quite wobbly. It did, however, prove very expensive to run. For this reason, it caused Laird

Montgomery a great deal of worry.

Being so old, the castle needed a lot of repair, most of which he could not afford. Carpets that were once red were worn through to their white threads. Curtains were faded and smelt like old socks, and the roof could only be described as being as holey as Swiss cheese. Rain puddles on the castle floors were not uncommon.

To make matters worse, many of the bills went unpaid, too. The castle no longer had electricity for this very reason. A rusty old generator, no larger than a shoebox, was used for essentials like the washing machine, and provided just enough power for half a cycle and no more. One side of their clothes remained dirty.

The lack of electricity also meant there was no lighting. And castles are very dark places to be, especially when the day's sun retreats. An inky blackness would set in then, robbing them of their sight.

In an attempt to resolve Drumtipperty's blackout, the corridors were lit with fire torches. Hundreds of years ago, these had been as large as a man's arm, but the ones that were now pinned to the walls were no bigger than a candle.

With only a trail of flickering light to guide them, the castle was grey, and it was gloomy. It was also downright spooky, especially with the odd happenings that had been occurring lately. Closed doors creaked open. Things were moved or misplaced. On three occasions, Hamish was sure he had seen the shadowy outline of what looked like a child far smaller than he, running along the stone corridors. Then, of course, there were the strange banging sounds that came from deep within the old dungeon after nightfall.

Those would make anyone's blood run cold.

2.

A New Plan for an Old Castle

"What you can hear is the broken boiler. It needs to be replaced. It's on my to-do list," Hamish's father would say of the strange *CREAK, CREAK, BANG, BANNNNG, BANG* noise, which could be heard most nights despite the boiler not being switched on.

Laird Montgomery's ever-growing to-do list now filled a bulging pocketbook. He carried this in his burgundy and cream check trousers along with a ballpoint pen. Any jobs that needed doing but could not be done until the castle's finances improved were entered and dated. *Replace boiler* was written down at least seventeen times.

The family tartan was something Laird Montgomery always wore. *Every. Single. Day.* And he insisted his son do the same. While the older of the two paired his with a woollen jumper, the younger chose to wear a hoodie, often with the hood up in protest against the imposed tartan dress code.

"We are Montgomerys. We are not going to be 'ordinary' and wear jeans! Honour your heritage!" his father would demand with a proud shake of his fist whenever Hamish brought up the mere possibility of wearing something else. The Laird would spout off about how special it was to come from an ancient Scottish family before concluding with the practicalities of such a fabric. "These tartan trews are made of wool," he would say. "They are far, far warmer than denim! They help keep our legs warm."

But Hamish's legs *never* felt warm. Because Drumtipperty Castle was cold. Bone-numbingly so. If you were to think of the coldest place you've ever been and multiply it by ten, it probably still wouldn't feel as cold as it did there.

Hamish felt it more than most. His bedroom was in the icy tip of the castle in the old turret. To get there, he had to cross a narrow, windowless stone landing and then follow a sixteen-step stone staircase that wound round in a tight spiral. The last step led to a tiny doorway that required anyone taller than five feet to stoop down to avoid knocking their head as they continued through.

For this reason, adults didn't often venture in. Hamish considered this very much an advantage when it came to cleaning, or not cleaning, his room or doing, or not doing, homework.

However, the curve of the room meant that not one piece of furniture sat flatly against the wall. With a bed, side table, wooden desk, and wardrobe, this made everything quite crowded. In fact, there wasn't much space for him to even move an elbow, which was the main contributing factor to Hamish's messy handwriting and poor homework scores. Or, at least, that's what he argued.

Unlike the other side of the castle, the old turret was entirely exposed. The south wing had been added to the original building much later, and its positioning was such that it was protected by a cloak of tall chestnut trees at the end of a big patch of grass known as the Grand Lawn. Today, of course, there was nothing grand about it. The once meticulously-striped lawn was overgrown, all life throttled out of it by weeds. Not the almost pretty, wild flower sort either, but the ugly, jaggy kind that spread like wildfire and stung or gave you a horrible weeping rash or blister should you brush against it with an exposed arm or leg.

Fortunately, this was not a common occurrence as shorts and T-shirts weather seldom came to Drumtipperty, and for the most part, it was cold. January, February, and early March brought the bleakest moments. Sheets of driving snow and rain fell like arrows from the sky, and gusts of Arctic wind would wrap around the turret, shaking it as vigorously as a maraca on especially blustery nights.

To keep warm, Hamish wore a pair of wooly socks under his pyjama bottoms and a scarf knotted around his neck. On the evenings that the temperature dipped well below zero, he had little choice but to invite Gorse into his bed.

"Please breathe the other way," the boy would instruct his giant dog, using a pillow to create a makeshift barrier between their faces. Sleeping in such close proximity to Gorse was hazardous – not only for the dog's musky breath, but also for his unfortunate habit of catapulting Hamish out of bed.

"Ahhhhhh!" Hamish would shout as he tumbled on to the floor with a thud while a snoring Gorse continued to pursue imaginary rats, long legs kicking frantically above.

Gorse was two years old, grey, and very large. His father had suggested he get a smaller dog, a spaniel of some kind, but no, he had wanted a Scottish deerhound, one of the tallest dogs there was.

After all, no one messed with someone who had

a big dog, did they? Not that there was anyone around for miles to have any sort of a disagreement with. Gorse wasn't especially vicious for that matter, either. In fact, he was probably one of the gentlest dogs you could find.

He was also very good at eating, a major plus point in itself. Gorse could be relied upon to devour all the food that his young owner didn't want to eat himself, which came in handy when dealing with the housekeeper's terrible cooking.

Therefore, it was only when the ten-year-old picked himself up from his bedroom floor, having been launched out of his bed for the third time in a night that he sometimes regretted his choice of pet. But only very briefly.

"Why don't we swap rooms?" Laird Montgomery had offered on several occasions and did so again one Sunday morning whilst the pair were eating toast and marmalade in the castle's kitchen.

In spite of another chilly night and two falls from his bed, Hamish declined. He knew his father had sore bones that seemed to stiffen up with the cold, and his own bedroom was unquestionably the coldest of all those in the castle. His father slept in the Green Room on the slightly warmer south side, where there were at least no indoor icicles. It had been named the Green Room according to the original green wallpaper that had been replaced with a yellow pineapple print long before either of them had been born.

"Things have been difficult, I know," began Laird Montgomery as he bit off a corner of toast and began to chew slowly.

The castle's kitchen was meant to be for cooking alone. As Montgomery family tradition dictated, the pair should have eaten their meals in the much grander but far colder dining room.

"Airs and graces won't keep us warm," his father would say as they seated themselves not at the fourteen foot mahogany table that was so shiny it was like eating off a mirror but at the old farmhouse bench, which was holey from woodworm and had pieces of cardboard sandwiched under its wobbly legs. Here in the kitchen, the glow of the log-burning fire warmed their backs. And that counted for a lot.

Having caught his third cold of the month, Hamish took a long slurp of his hot orange and watched Laird Montgomery push his spectacles up on to his forehead that had lined with age. His father's hair was more grey than it was brown.

Hamish had been five years old when Mrs Montgomery left without word of a goodbye. At precisely midday on the twelfth chime of the old grandfather clock, she tottered out of Drumtipperty Castle in red heels, carrying a small red suitcase that fitted no more than a single change of clothes. His father had not been the same since.

"I've been doing a lot of thinking – how the castle can make some money," said the Laird as he took a sip from a chipped mug filled with grey, watery-looking tea.

Drumtipperty Castle had been playing on his mind a lot lately. The castle had fallen into serious disrepair. They could barely afford to keep the place running, and its size and upkeep had become a gigantic burden. A black cloud of worry followed him around almost every day.

"I don't want to pass on a sinking ship, and this ship – this castle, is doing just that. We need money," continued the Laird. "We need money...to survive. So I've had an idea."

Hamish was only half-listening. Munching on a large mouthful of buttered toast himself and blowing his nose like a trumpet, he remembered he had not yet done a whole weekend's worth of homework set by his teacher, Governess Stewart.

As there were no schools within a ninety-minute drive of Drumtipperty, Hamish was home schooled. This was not as fun or as easy as it sounds. Although Governess Stewart only taught him three days a week, she set lots of homework to fill, what felt like, every single minute of the other days. Nor did she teach sports, the very thing he was best at.

"You'll be able to play rugby, football and hockey at Graceford," she reminded him with arched eyebrows whenever he complained of doing yet more equations and spellings.

Hamish was to be sent to Graceford Scottish School of Perfection next year to study and board. The boys only boarding school was almost 200 miles away. Laird Montgomery had gone there, and so had his father, and his father before that. Montgomerys went to Graceford, and that was that.

"So my idea is this." Laird Montgomery paused again, allowing Hamish to finish blowing his nose, which was becoming redder by the second. "I've decided that, after 874 years, Drumtipperty Castle is opening its doors to the public – the PAYING public."

Hamish stopped chewing. "The public?" he asked doubtfully, his mouth still full of mushed-up toast. He wondered whether or not this idea was a serious one. His father didn't much like the public. In fact, he had been known to call them trespassing idiots and chase them off the estate with a shotgun.

"It's part of my plan to save Drumtipperty," said the Laird, sensing his son's surprise. He had already torn down the *PRIVATE – BY APPOINTMENT ONLY* and *TRESPASSERS*

BEWARE – YOU WILL BE SHOT signs from the castle's entrance. Next on the agenda was to move a few things out of the castle's small reception room. Laird Montgomery imagined the vegans may not like Albert, the stuffed stag head, or Cornelius, the four-foot salmon, that were currently mounted on the wall down there.

Unsure what to say to such a proposal, Hamish started chewing again, his mouth not quite closed.

"Just you wait, son!" said his father with more enthusiasm than he had shown in a very long time. "I can feel it in my water. Things are about to change for the better!"

They continued eating their toast with the hope this was true. But plans don't always go to plan as Laird Montgomery would shortly discover. And things were not yet to get better.

3.

A Peculiar Discovery

Lady Foo Foo Archer moved into Drumtipperty shortly after and proved to be a dreadful houseguest in terms of appetite, toilet habits, and staying well beyond her welcome. Not that anyone had invited her in the first place.

Hamish was the one to make the discovery. He shouldn't have because he was specifically told to keep out of the drawing room where she had taken up residence.

"There's no reason for you to be in that room," the Laird had warned him sternly. "I'm storing some important antiques in there, and I don't want them damaged."

Admittedly, Hamish was not someone you wanted around expensive one-off pieces. He was the sort of boy who tripped and fell and, to avoid knocking over something, would then knock over another three things. A blue and white Chinese vase, a coloured glass lamp, and a walnut wood clock had all fallen victim to his clumsy footing in the past.

In his defence, the day he ventured into the

drawing room he had been especially bored. The kind of bored that seemed impossible to escape no matter how hard he tried. The kind of bored that usually landed him in trouble.

It had been raining heavily all morning, and Hamish and Gorse had been stuck indoors for what felt like an eternity and then some. They had played ball inside and smashed not one, but two crystal glasses. They had raced up all the sets of stairs on the north side of the castle before racing down all the sets of stairs on the south side, too. They had made an obstacle course with different pieces of furniture and timed how long it took to complete. They had then used the same furniture to make hurdles for their corridor race and timed that, too. By 11:45am, Hamish was struggling to think of what else they could possibly do that didn't require more furniture or indeed some form of electricity.

Deciding it was too early for lunch at 11:46am, he went in search of some further entertainment and, trying the door handle of the drawing room en route to his own bedroom, discovered it opened. *How strange*, thought Hamish. This room was always, always locked. Laird Montgomery made sure of that. He kept the drawing room key in a small wooden box that was also locked in his locked study.

The boy threw a quick look over his right shoulder and then his left. No one was around. He slipped through the *creaking* door unnoticed with Gorse trotting closely behind.

The drawing room would have been almost grand if it weren't for piles and piles of boxes, stacks of chairs, and other bits and pieces of random furniture scattered around. It all looked like a jumble sale. Hamish had to turn sideways and breathe in just to squeeze past a stack of books and a chest filled with things wrapped in newspaper. There were also boxes – dozens of them, some taped up, others crammed so full their lids gaped open.

To the top of the room was a huge white stone fireplace and an even bigger painting above that, about six feet tall, with a thick, gold frame. From his father's many stories, Hamish instantly recognised the angry looking man in it as his ancestor Angus Montgomery, a fearless warrior who had fought and won many a battle in Scotland and lost a finger in the process.

Angus was an earl and a clan chieftain, making him part of the nobility at the time. Not only was he featured in several Scottish history books, he had his own Wikipedia page, too.

The painting was dark and murky looking, the sort of colour you get when you mix a dirty paintbrush in a pot of water. Dressed head to toe in the Montgomery tartan, Angus sat on a white horse. In his right hand, he grasped a giant black sword as if preparing to plunge it into the head of an enemy soldier and cleave him in two. His left hand was missing the middle finger.

While Gorse stretched out in the only free corner of floor that wasn't taken up by boxes, Hamish decided to rummage through a few of them – just the open ones. He wasn't sure what he was searching for, but he had a peculiar feeling he should be finding something important.

His search was well underway when he first heard the noise. Or at least he thought he did. By the time he freed his head and arms of the box, it had all gone quiet again. He scanned the room, waiting amongst the sea of cardboard for a follow-up – some sort of secondary noise to prove he hadn't just imagined the first one. Gorse briefly lifted his head before returning it to the floor.

Still nothing. Only pellets of rain being fired against the window as the torrential downpour continued outside.

Maybe he just thought he'd heard something, he decided, and pushed his head and shoulders back into the box, stretching all the way down to reach for something round and shiny at the bottom.

There it was again. What was it? A rustling or something. It didn't sound like the old boiler which, besides, was only heard at night.

Feeling uneasy, Hamish began to put everything back although probably not as carefully as he should, and things were dropped into a different box than they were in before. His eyes glanced back to the fireplace. Was he imagining it or had the painting changed? The sharp point of Angus's sword now seemed to be pointing directly at him. No, it must have been like that before. He was simply looking at it from a different angle. He definitely *was* imagining it.

Or was he? As he stared at the canvas, the blacks, browns and reds seemed to swirl together, then stop, then move some more, and stop. Hamish wondered if it was like one of those magic eye pictures, that if you stared long enough, it all blurred together to produce some secret image underneath.

"WOOF, WOOF, WOOF!"

The deerhound's barks broke his concentration, and with a start, he fell out of the trance he had slipped into. "Be quiet, Gorse!" he hushed crossly, not wanting to alert Laird Montgomery or Mrs Cook, the castle's housekeeper, of their whereabouts.

"WOOF, WOOF, WOOF!"

"What is it Gorse?"

"WOOF!"

Gorse, now fully awake from his slumber, was crouched before the drawing room's large bay window, wagging his tail furiously.

"What is it?"

Mottled with patches of black mould, the red and gold tasselled curtains hung like weights. Despite their great heft, the one on the left was billowing back and forth, so much so that it was stirring up puffs of grey dust from the floor.

There was something behind it.

Hamish crept closer, his heartbeat quickening as the curtain continued to sway to and fro.

He was about to snatch it back when, like a performer revealing itself on stage, one short leg paraded out, then the other; each had a claw.

The ten-year-old had never seen a bird like it. And he knew the names of most. A keen naturalist, he could identify everything from a goldfinch and wren to a blackbird and jackdaw, and recite their scientific names, too.

This particular bird was blue and vibrantly so, and it had a long tail feather similar to that of a pheasant.

At first, Hamish felt relieved that it was just a bird and not something else. Like a ghost. And a ghost wasn't unfeasible given the strange things that had occurred in the castle over the last few weeks. But then he began fretting. *How would it get out? Would it fly against the window and damage its wings? Would it starve to death?* In his head, he ran through a handful of awful scenarios and got more upset for the bird's welfare with every passing thought.

Hamish was a worrier. He found himself worrying about lots of stuff and would spend many hours needlessly overthinking things – things he couldn't possibly change.

On top of that, he liked ALL animals and

insects, even the ones other people didn't. Like seagulls, spiders, mice and forky tails. Though he had yet to encounter them, he imagined he would very much like snakes, crocodiles, sharks and hyenas.

"Animal daft, at's fit ye are. We shid be ca'ing ye Hamish Attenborough!" Mrs Cook would tell him every time he rescued an insect from the kitchen sink that she would otherwise flush down the plughole.

Hamish, therefore, immediately took it upon himself to help the blue bird out. He was duty-bound. But despite his best efforts to lure the strange creature outside, it insisted on holding its ground. Even when he fetched some of Mrs Cook's bread from the kitchen and laid a trail of crumbs out the door, the bird simply gobbled up all those inside the drawing room and refused to cross the open doorway.

Hamish returned the next day and the one after that, too, quietly revisiting for two weeks straight. Each time the drawing room door was not only unlocked, it seemed to swing open of its own accord. Before he even raised a hand.

He brought fresh water and seeds. Mrs Cook kept a large stock of them in the castle's larder. She liked to use them for a crunchy topping on her disgusting, Marmite and beef stock muffins.

Along with the in-room dining, he made a delivery of fresh towels – the better guest ones that weren't thread-worn. Having constructed a very comfortable fluffy nest-bed, the ten-year-old found these required daily replacement, such was the bird's capacity to poo. Meanwhile the dirty ones were scooped up and bundled into the washing machine to be half-washed and then half-washed again.

Hamish told no one of his discovery. After all,

he was bound to get in trouble for being somewhere he shouldn't. So for now, the bird's mysterious appearance remained a secret.

4.

The Flying Carpet Bomber

Laird Montgomery had come in search of a silver antique he thought he might sell to pay for a new washing machine or for a plumber to fix the old one that had just broken due to some sort of clogging issue. The eighteenth century jug, which had been in his family for hundreds of years, was not something he wanted to part with, but he felt having clean underpants was necessary.

The drawing room door was always locked. It was something he insisted on. There were many valuables inside, and he could not afford for anything to be damaged or go missing, not in these penniless times.

Pulling a small bronze key from his pocket, he popped it in the lock and turned. The handle did not move. He tried again, but the door was quite stuck as if someone was on the other side gripping the handle. Feeling annoyed that this was going to take far longer than the eight minutes and fifty-seven seconds he had allocated to complete the task, he pushed the handle down even harder so that it made his hand go blotchy.

"Come on, you useless thing!"

After a fierce tug and an almighty shove, the door suddenly opened. Laird Montgomery fell into the drawing room. Off flew his glasses.

"Argggggghhh," he cried out as he struck two boxes before landing on the floor with a considerable *WALLOP*.

"Idiot door! Idiot boxes! Idiot floor!" he muttered from his knees and swiped his arms around in search of his glasses. He could see very little, if anything, without them.

When he did find them three minutes later, they felt slimy, and when he pushed them on to his face, he couldn't see any more than he did without them. Everything was white, like a snowstorm.

"What on earth is going on?" he mumbled to himself, removing the spectacles to wipe them along his tartan trouser leg, not seeing the long, white streak they had left behind.

It was when he returned them to his face for a second time that he saw it – white spatters of what looked like both wet and dried paint, everywhere:

over the sofas, the fireplace, the rug, the antique table, the clock, the boxes. Even the painting of his great-great-great-great-great-great-grandfather, Angus Montgomery, had a white mark projecting from his nose as if he had sneezed out a very large bogey.

Except all of this wasn't paint. Or bogies.

But what it was, he was unsure.

Deciding to investigate, he took several steps towards the fireplace.

"WOAH, WOAH, WOAH," he shouted, slipping on a patch of the unidentified white stuff and crashing to the floor.

A soft tinkle of laughter rang out somewhere behind him.

The Laird swung around.

No one was there.

Thankful his glasses were still on his face, he pushed himself back up. Yet he was soon off his feet when he slipped again. This time his legs went in opposite directions before his bottom smacked painfully off the ground.

More laughter. A child's laugh.

Whipping his head around, he expected to see Hamish, but his son was nowhere in sight. Instead, he spotted a strange blue bird balancing on top of the window's gold curtain rail.

"What the…"

There was no time for him to utter a cuss word before it made its descent. An explosion of white droppings hit the floor and his green woollen jumper.

"ARRRRHHHHHH!"

Shielding his head with his hands, the Laird rolled on to his stomach. Blue wings whistled through the air. A downpour followed as the bird undertook its second dive bomb.

SPLATTER, SPLATTER, SPLATTER,

SPLATTER.

"AHHHHHHHHHHH!"

To avoid a third poo pelting, the castle owner decided he needed an escape plan. Cupping his hands to his eyes as if they were binoculars, he scoped possible exit routes. If he could make it to the boxes on the far corner of the drawing room, he could navigate around the back of them and out the door.

Using his elbows to carry his weight, he began army crawling. He managed to reach the old antique table and took cover underneath it. Emptying the contents of a nearby cardboard box with a *CLATTER*, the Laird pulled it over his head in preparation for the next onslaught of poop and continued blindly dragging himself along the floor, bumping into objects along the way.

"Ouch, ah, ouch, ah, ouch."

Eventually reaching the heavy drawing room door, he knew it was now or never. This bird was not going to cease-fire.

"One, two, three," he panted and ripped the cardboard box off his head while grappling with the handle at the same time. It didn't budge. He tugged again, his panic mounting as the blue creature circled the ceiling above, preparing once again to offload its bowel.

Then, with another great heave, the door finally gave way, and Laird Montgomery fell through into the carpeted corridor, his body caked in white slime.

As bad luck would have it, Hamish was turning the corner at that very moment with an armful of towels and seed supplies.

The bird droppings had started becoming a problem about four days ago. Hamish had tried to clean it up at first, but with more and more appearing every day by the hour, he couldn't quite keep on top of it. He had since resorted to wearing his raincoat and tying plastic carrier bags over his shoes.

Before the ten-year-old had a chance to change direction, the Laird prised open a poo-encrusted eyelid, and Hamish knew there and then that this was one of those days where he had landed himself in trouble.

5.

Bird Man

"Crikey, I'm not an early bird!" said Mr Guillemot to no one but himself as he pushed down the car accelerator with such force that he almost detached his neck from his shoulders.

The Scottish Bird Protection Unit officer was running very late. When he eventually pulled up to Drumtipperty Castle in an old, battered blue car, spluttering a trail of grey smoke like a steam train, it was 3:55pm; not 1pm as agreed.

This annoyed Laird Montgomery no end. If there was one thing he could not stand it was lateness. He was a man who liked his day to run like clockwork. Whether it was an important meeting with the bank, doing the castle's accounts, drinking a cup of tea or even going to the toilet – he allocated a certain amount of time for everything.

To maintain such an orderly schedule, the Laird wore two watches – one strapped to each wrist. On his left was an eighteen-carat gold antique pocket watch that had been made into a wristwatch with the addition of a brown leather strap. On his right, hidden under the cuff of his jumper, he wore a black plastic battery-powered watch that cost £11.99 and came from China. This was in the event that the antique watch stopped working, which was every other day.

For the last three hours, the Laird had checked both watches fifteen times. He angrily tapped the glass of the old antique watch with his finger, convinced it must have stopped, only to check the plastic one, which confirmed both the time and the lateness of his guest.

When Mr Guillemot did eventually arrive, it took him a further ten minutes to park. This was despite there not being another single car in a driveway large enough to accommodate five coaches at one time.

To begin with, he swung in front-first. He then decided to reverse back and reposition the car, but ended up driving forward to the exact same spot where he had originally parked. After turning off his engine and sitting stationary for two full minutes, he decided to move again, this time reversing back at full speed and spinning his steering wheel hard to the left, so the car made a whizzing arc shape, a bit like a firework.

VROOOOOOOOM. EEEEEEEKKKKKKK. The car's brakes screeched loudly, stopping him from careering into the side of the castle.

Having come to a sudden halt, there was a horrible crunching sound, *ERRRRRRRR, ERRRRRR*, as he tried to find first gear. The little blue car then did an entire loop of the parking bay with its engine revving noisily. Only after completing a second loop did he finally decide to park his car slap bang in the middle of the gravelled driveway, partially blocking the entrance and making it impossible for any other vehicle to park without driving over a corner of lawn. Unbuckling his seatbelt, he climbed out.

Laird Montgomery watched the whole episode from his study window, aghast. "Absolute idiot," he groaned and wondered what the next hour of his visitor's company would bring.

6.

Birds will be Birds

Mr Guillemot was an ornithologist. A bird specialist, in simpler terms. He was a short man whose navy blue hooded raincoat was far too big for him; it reached down to his knees rather than his waist. Strapped to his back was a huge rucksack that was about half of his total body size. He also wore a pair of big black boots and a large set of binoculars around his neck, which bounced off his chest whenever he took a step forward.

"Apologies, I had another bird crisis involving a trapped heron to attend to first," he said when he finally appeared at the castle door, dressed as if he were setting off to trek the Amazon rainforest. "It's all been a bit of a rush today. I am a bit out of breath! You could say I'm PUFFIN!"

Mr Guillemot paused, waiting for laughter. But Laird Montgomery's lips remained clamped shut. He was not in the mood for jokes, especially not anything bird-related given the circumstances. Rather than laughing or replying at all, he offered a handshake, which was returned without any grip. This annoyed the Laird even more. As well as a strict timekeeper, he was a man who liked a firm handshake. Anything less than a solid squeeze was simply not good enough.

"This is the way," directed the Laird as he guided his visitor through the heavy wooden door – the kind that was only ever found on a castle. Adorned with sharp, black metal studs, and no bell or knocker, it was distinctly unwelcoming, as a castle door should be.

"Very cosy," said Mr Guillemot of the fire in the

reception hall, which had been put on several hours ago especially for him and had all but burned out. Only one orange ember remained in a pile of black ash.

The bird protection officer was led up the first flight of stone stairs and off to the right, along the wide carpeted corridor known as the 'gallery'. This, along with the drawing room, was by far the grandest part of the castle, and was filled with paintings of people's faces, racks of rifles, stuffed stag heads and sword displays fanned out on the wall. It was here that Hamish joined the two men.

As they inched towards the drawing room, the castle owner noticed Mr Guillemot's boots were covered in mud, presumably from the heron rescue earlier that day. With every step, a large clump of earth fell from the thick black soles, muddying the floor wherever they went.

Thinking of the time that would now have to

be designated to tidy up it all up, the Laird's face clouded over.

Hamish saw it, as did Mr Guillemot, who stopped so abruptly that his backpack thumped into his head and almost knocked him flat off his feet.

"Messy business – being the SAS of the wildlife world," chuckled the bird officer as he began removing his boots. Or attempting to. With his bag weighing him down, this was a bit of a balancing act. It kept sliding to one side, threatening to pull him over with its ample weight. What precisely required such a large backpack that didn't involve an around-the-world expedition was a mystery to Laird Montgomery.

"If you don't mind…?" Mr Guillemot gestured towards his feet, having hopped and stumbled for a third time without successfully removing either boot.

This day is getting worse by the minute, silently fumed the Laird as he crouched down to assist.

Not only did it take a full five minutes and forty-five seconds of heaving before the boots were wrestled from Mr Guillemot's sweaty feet, but the man also had two giant holes in his damp, mismatched socks. During the boot extraction, a toe with a curled, yellowing nail prodded the Laird squarely on his forehead.

Worse still, in the time it took to untie the tightly criss-crossed laces of both boots, Mr Guillemot had told three more bird jokes.

Hamish could see his father was getting more and more irritated with every punchline. Nonetheless, he decided this was as good an opportunity as any to tell his own bird joke – the one about a woodpecker with no beak.

"A headbanger! You call it a headbanger!"

Mr Guillemot's body shook with laugher,

causing the boots, now in his hands, to shower the floor with powdery mud. "PWAHAHAAHA! You really QUACK me up, Hamish. You really do!"

By now, seven minutes and thirty-nine seconds had been wasted, and Laird Montgomery was struggling to contain his rage. Consulting his plastic watch once more, he seized the drawing room door.

Nothing happened. Again, it appeared to be stuck.

"I don't understand. The door was unlocked..."

As he bent his elbow in preparation for a second, more violent attempt, Hamish slipped underneath and grabbed the handle himself. The door immediately swung open.

"So the bird is in here?" asked Mr Guillemot whilst craning his long neck around the doorframe.

"Yes, it is," Laird Montgomery replied,

wondering how on earth his son had managed to open the door. "I'm not sure what kind it is, but it's blue and vicious!"

Mr Guillemot followed Hamish inside. Laird Montgomery entered last. Producing a newspaper from under his arm, he held it above his head like a tent.

"My things! THAT BLASTED BIRD!" he cried as they surveyed the mess.

The drawing room remained as before. Absolutely everything was covered in bird poo.

"Birds will be birds," said Mr Guillemot with a knowing nod. "We all need to go to the bathroom. Some of us more than others," he added, remembering he needed to use a toilet himself having swigged two cans of Irn-Bru during his three-hour car journey to Drumtipperty Castle.

Putting his full bladder out of his mind, Mr Guillemot got to work. With the bird nowhere in sight, he began examining the droppings, rubbing some between his thumb and forefinger and giving it a good sniff.

"You do know that bird poo actually has a very important job? It fertilises the ground. Although it's not such good news inside, of course, should it land on anything. Bird poo eats away at things, eventually dissolving it to nothing. I've seen lots of statues missing heads, arms, and various other appendages because of bird droppings!"

Once Mr Guillemot had rattled off the many things he'd seen destroyed by bird poo, he cupped his hands to his mouth and started making odd noises. Laird Montgomery thought this hardly hygienic given the white smears across his hands.

"Tea-cher, Tea-cher, Tea-cher, Tea-cher," Mr Guillemot called out.

"Chiff-chaff, chiff-chaff, chiff-chaff."

"Deeeedeeeedeeeeerdecuuuuuupa."

"Twit-twit-twit-twit-twit."

"What is this idiot doing?" cursed the Laird under his breath as the bird officer continued making one strange noise after the next while Hamish attempted to memorise them all.

"Warble, warble, warble, warble."

"Rarararakkkkkkeeee."

Exhausting a total of 107 birdcalls, Mr Guillemot looked at a loss as to what to do next. Hamish suggested the bird was behind the big red curtain, but the wildlife officer insisted it should come out of its own accord.

"You said it was a blue bird, didn't you? Well, I'm not sure this will work, but let's give it a try," Mr Guillemot said, having an idea. "Foooobay, foooobay, banyayayayaya, banyayayaya, carrrrocha, foooobay, banyayayaya, carrrocha."

Immediately, there was a rustling behind the fabric of the curtains, and a blue-feathered head with two beady black eyes popped out, giving them all a good glare.

"Well, I never, that's a Lady Foo Foo Archer," gasped Mr Guillemot, appearing like he may faint. "She's come back from the dead!"

7.

Not an Eagle or a Falcon

"Lady WHO?" demanded Laird Montgomery, having never heard of such a bird or indeed a person by that name.

"Lady Foo Foo Archer. A type of pheasant – an extinct pheasant, or so we thought! This bird hasn't been seen in Scotland for hundreds of years!" said Mr Guillemot, his hands shaking with excitement. "It's quite incredible! A miracle even! It's a female because of its blue feathers and tail plumes."

Without taking off his backpack, Mr Guillemot reached a long arm around and unzipped a side pocket to produce a grey electronic device that was about the size of a tablet and had two little metal antennas sprouting out the top and wires coming out the side.

"What's that?"

"This, Hamish, is a BB101 – the most specialist bird technology known to man. The NASA of the bird world! I have all the information ever known about every species of bird that has ever lived stored on this device."

Mr Guillemot started selecting files from the blue screen. "Aha, here she is, Lady Foo Foo Archer. Originally native to the Chinese uplands and its bamboo forests, she was brought across the seas by a famous Italian merchant. He named the pheasant after a very rich Scottish woman called Lady Foo Foo Archer, whom he then presented to as a gift. The woman tried to breed the exotic pheasant with an equally rare hunting eagle she had received from another love interest in hope of combining the patriotic blue colour of one bird and the aggressive fighting spirit of the other. This blue hybrid bird would be then used on the battlefield to peck out the eyes of enemies."

Laird Montgomery threw a nervous look in Lady Foo Foo Archer's direction, whose beak continued to poke out from the side of the curtain.

"Is that what killed them all?" asked Hamish. "The battles?"

Mr Guillemot shook his head. "No, it would seem the African eagle and Lady Foo Foo Archer couldn't stand one another. Hated each other's guts the second they laid eyes on each other and refused to be mates. The problem was only a blue female from China and a male eagle from Africa had been shipped across. Eventually, nature took its course."

"Oh," said the 10-year-old. "So that was it, then?"

"Not quite." The ornithologist began swiping up more files from the screen. "According to this, the two birds were separated because of their squabbling. Deciding she liked the African merchant better, the woman sent the blue bird to her second cousin's estate, where someone tried to steal it from the grounds of the castle. After that, the blue bird was kept inside for her own safety and became a pet. When she died of old age a few years later, the family were so upset by their loss, they added the bird's design to the family's coat of arms as a tribute."

"Madness. Utter madness," remarked Laird Montgomery who was now using his newspaper to flick off some bird droppings that had gathered on the sole of his shoe.

The wildlife protection officer paused and looked up from the small blue screen. "'Madness' it may be, Mr Montgomery, but it would appear such madness is something your family is quite familiar with."

The Laird looked up from his rolled newspaper, outraged. "I beg your pardon?!"

"If the evidence is correct, the Scottish estate who took Lady Foo Foo Archer in, is Drumtipperty – and she is the very bird who graces your coat of arms!"

Their shoeless visitor said the last part with the sort of flourish a barrister might when winning a courtroom argument.

"What?" squawked the Laird.

"Apparently so." Mr Guillemot tapped the screen under his fingers. "That's what the research points to. The BB101 is 101 per cent accurate – that's where the machine gets its name from."

The castle owner's mouth gaped open like a caught fish. "I… I… I…no, that can't be. No, certainly not! The one on our family crest is something predatory, like an eagle or a falcon, not an idiot pheasant!"

"A Chinese pheasant, to be precise!"

"I don't care where the idiot thing came from!" said the Laird, pulling at the arm of his woollen jumper to cover up the black plastic watch peeking out from under his sleeve. "I just want to know why it is in my drawing room all these years later!"

"As do I," said the bird protection officer, now adopting the air of a police constable. "That was my next question. Have you been running an illegal breeding programme at Drumtipperty, Mr Montgomery?"

The Laird responded by making a choking noise.

"Under the Wildlife and Countryside Act (1981), it is not permitted to breed and release non-native birds into the British countryside," Mr Guillemot cautioned.

"WHAT?" screeched the castle owner. "ARE YOU HAVING A LAUGH? ALL MY MOST TREASURED PROPERTY IS COVERED IN BIRD TURDS, AND YOU ARE ASKING ME IF I'M THE ONE WHO IS RESPONSIBLE!"

The ornithologist rubbed his bearded chin thoughtfully. "There is something in the bird world we call iterative evolution."

Hamish and the Laird looked blankly at their guest.

"It's the evolution of a species from a common ancestor which repeats at different times in history so that the species can evolve itself back into existence," explained Mr Guillemot. "It is uncommon but not unheard of. A case occurred last year on an island in the Indian Ocean. So it's certainly not outside the realms of possibility. But how she ended up inside your drawing room is quite the puzzler. Do you leave the windows open in here?"

"No, never," said the Laird between gritted teeth. "They are jammed shut. I can't even open them with a metal wrench. Believe me, I've tried. The door is kept locked at all times, too. I'm the only one who has a key, and I'm *the only one* who is allowed in here." He shot Hamish a purposeful look when he said the last bit.

"Well, she has decided to make her home here, nonetheless, and that we must respect," said Mr Guillemot.

The Laird lowered his voice conspiringly. "Yes, yes, I respect that. I do. But how am I going to get the blasted thing out? What can I do to get rid of it?"

Having brought out a large laptop from his backpack and plugged it into the BB101, the bird protection officer was too busy tapping the keys to answer. After a moment or two, the computer started making a loud beeping noise.

Snapping the lid shut with a bang, he shook his head. "Nothing, I'm afraid. Nothing can be done. I've just entered the details into our database. The bird has officially been reintroduced to our red list of protected species."

"What does that mean?" asked the castle owner impatiently.

"It means Lady Foo Foo Archer has gone from dead-as-a-dodo to back-from-the-dead-but-for-how-long-who-knows. It means she is staying put for the time being."

"Staying put? Staying put? I need to open this room up to the paying public. I can't be showing them a dangerous bird and a room decorated in poo!" cried the Laird.

Mr Guillemot shrugged. "You could get a professional in to open up the windows and hope she leaves. But while Lady Foo Foo Archer is on your property, it is your responsibility to continue feeding her and not to disturb her chosen habitat. She is once again a protected species. I'm sure she will vacate when she is good and ready."

"When *she* is good and ready?" With his temper rising, Laird Montgomery was repeating everything like some sort of demented parrot. If he were a cartoon character, Hamish reckoned, steam would be pouring out of his father's ears about now. "You don't understand. We are opening to the public in less than four weeks."

"I'm afraid there really is nothing to be done," said Mr Guillemot, his own patience starting to wear thin as he slotted his laptop and the BB101 into the rucksack, which he had not once removed from his back the entire time. "That bird is back on the critical list. It's an offence to do anything that may endanger the species."

"But it's already endangered! It's on the brink

of extinction, and it doesn't have a mate," argued the Laird. "So it's a goner!"

"Laird Montgomery, I'm telling you to leave that bird well alone. You will be issued with a large fine should anything happen to it – that I will make sure of."

Zipping up all the open pockets on his bag whilst still wearing it, Mr Guillemot changed his voice so it sounded softer and more polite. "Now, once you've helped me with my footwear, do you mind if I use your bathroom? I have a long journey ahead of me for my next appointment. I am afraid a sick robin is in serious need of some tweetment!"

8.

The Stolen Sword

As much as it annoyed Laird Montgomery, he had little choice but to allow Hamish to continue feeding Lady Foo Foo Archer. He could not afford a fine from the Scottish Bird Protection Unit. Nor could he afford to fix the windows. So, for the time being, the bird was indeed staying put.

Other than immediately evicting the idiotic creature, he decided the next best thing was to shift his belongings out of the drawing room and store them elsewhere until the castle tours got underway and the antiques would be put on display for the public.

During their 874 years, the Montgomerys had

accumulated various pieces of gold, silver, china, pottery and metalwork. Of course, some were worth more than others. Had the castle still been in possession of the Montgomery Claymore, he imagined their fortunes would have been quite different. They certainly wouldn't be turning their underpants inside out to get a second wear out of them.

The Montgomery Claymore was a sword unlike any other. Forged by a royal blacksmith in steel that was so strong it seemingly turned black, it had been made for Angus Montgomery, one of the fiercest fighters Scotland had ever known.

"The claymore was so long and so heavy that most men had neither the height nor the strength to wield it," his grandfather Donald had told him when he was a boy not much older than Hamish. "But your great-great-great-great-great-great-great-grandfather, the Earl, was a giant of a man who stood over seven and a half feet tall with shoulders the size of boulders."

To illustrate that point, his grandfather had led him into the drawing room where a colossal painting of a man with sky blue eyes, brown hair, and a fiery red beard scowled down. The picture showed the Earl from the waist up, sitting on a white horse and wielding a huge black sword. One hand was missing a middle finger.

"Look, the Earl was so tall, the artist couldn't fit his whole body inside the frame!"

The elderly man pointed a long, bony finger upwards as if it were his own sword. "Legend says in battle, the claymore's black steel would glow like a hot poker and burn the eyes of its enemies. Blinding them all!"

As a young boy, Laird Montgomery had been as curious about this magical sword as he was frightened. But when he asked to see it, he was met with his grandfather's long wagging finger.

"You can't," he said, shaking his head. "You can't!"

"Why not?" demanded the young Laird, prepared to argue his case.

"Because it's gone, boy. The claymore is gone."

"Gone?"

"Yes, gone, gone forever. Stolen. It was taken from the castle one winter's night. In all our history, not one enemy had breached the doors of Drumtipperty, and here we were, burgled by a bunch of petty thieves!" The old man shook with anger, even all those years later. "I was thirteen at the time. We didn't hear a thing, not a peep. In fact, not one person in the castle stirred until 11 a.m. the next morning, which was very odd. I thought our cook, Mrs Burwick, was in on it. That she perhaps drugged our pheasant stew..."

"Where should I put this?"

Laird Montgomery was still thinking of his grandfather, the Earl, and the black steel sword when Hamish appeared with the first of many boxes. He hadn't yet told his son about the claymore but would do so as soon as the boy began showing an interest in the castle's history.

"Over there, please." Laird Montgomery thumbed in the direction of the cobbled courtyard, which sat in the very middle of the castle with the tower and the rest of the castle's grey stone buildings surrounding it. The courtyard's outer walls, known as a curtain wall, had once acted as a form of defence to prevent enemy soldiers from getting inside the castle itself.

How a formerly extinct blue pheasant had managed to wander through the courtyard, through a bolted door, and then through another locked door to get into the drawing room, unnoticed, was a mystery to say the least.

With the clear-up operation now well underway, a basin filled to the brim with seeds and bread had been placed below the fireplace to entice their greedy blue guest. Lady Foo Foo Archer liked her grub as much as she liked doing number twos. And it was hoped this edible decoy would allow them to move the slimy white boxes outside and on to the back courtyard to be cleaned without fear of further explosive poo attacks.

According to Mr Guillemot, bird droppings could be toxic. Precautions had been taken. Faces were masked and hands were gloved, so one might assume they were handling a deadly nerve agent. Meanwhile, the drawing room door had been wedged open with one of the many boxes.

"I don't want it playing silly beggars again," said the Laird, or at least that's what it sounded like. The white mask that looped around his ears and covered his mouth muffled his words every time he gave an instruction.

Hamish was on his sixth trip to collect boxes when he decided, without doubt, that something very odd was happening to the giant painting of Earl Angus.

"Don't be ludicrous!" was the Laird's response when he first mentioned it at the beginning of the clear up, however. "It must be the sunlight coming in and out of the clouds and bouncing off the canvas that makes the claymore appear like it's changing. Now stop gawping and get on with the task at hand. We're already running almost four minutes behind schedule!"

But the boy was convinced otherwise. He was sure the sword in Earl Angus's hand kept switching from an ash black to a molten silver and then back, each time he stepped in and out of the room.

And that wasn't all.

The background of the painting looked different, too. A tree had now appeared in the left corner of the portrait. It looked very much like the old oak in the outer grounds of the castle, a big brute of a tree that was as almost as wide as it was tall. Over the years, the oak had become his nemesis. When it came to climbing it, the tree seemed to conspire against him, and he found it impossible to get any further than the ninth branch, *even* when adopting the monkey scruncher, a specialist swing and grab technique he had developed for when branches are set too wide apart.

While Hamish took a break to inspect the painting, Laird Montgomery was making headway outside. He intended to use a garden hose to speed up the cleaning process. *A little sprinkling of water was what everything needed,* he thought as he unravelled the long green piping across the courtyard.

After gently placing a dozen antiques on the ground to avoid any small chips, he fixed the hose to the outdoor tap and spun it on. At first, there was nothing, not a single drop of water. The hose then made a stuttering sound like the noise someone makes when they have a piece of food stuck in their throat before...

WHOOOOSH!

The water blasted out like a cannon.

CRASH! SMASH! CRASH! SMASH! CRASH! SMASH! CRASH! SMASH!

Armed with the hose, the Laird knocked two rows of antiques flat over. They fell like skittles, each shattering one after the other.

"ARGHHHH, IDIOT HOSE!" he yelled in despair at the mountain of broken china and glass. Evidently, this quick-fire method of cleaning was not going to work after all. The antiques would have to be cleaned by hand instead. *More blasted time*, he thought.

Yet, the garden hose seemed to have other ideas. When Laird Mongomery tried to drop it, he discovered he couldn't. He just couldn't. It stayed clamped to the palms of his hands like a machine gun, firing out more and more water. Even more peculiarly, it started veering to the left, taking aim at the next row of old jugs and chinaware. As the Laird attempted, with all his might to push it back over, the hose began to leap around in his hands, thrashing from side to side like he was in an arm-wrestling contest with an unknown contestant and losing. Gallons of water splashed around, bouncing off the cobbles and showering him in the process. It was only when it threatened to pull him off his feet entirely that he released his grip.

The hose fell. For a moment, it lay flat on the ground, continuing to spew out water.

Then something weirder happened. The long green pipe began to rise up. Slowly, it snaked from side to side as if it was hypnotised, its metal nozzle glinting in the sun.

The Laird rubbed his eyes. Was he going mad? Yes, he must be. How could he explain this otherwise?

Suddenly and without warning, the hose nose-dived and lashed the ground by his feet. And the castle owner was left with no choice but to jump. Then jump and jump again as it continued to circle his feet faster and faster. *Yes, I must be going mad*, he thought as he skipped the green piping. His shoes, which were now soaked through, made a horrible squelching noise. Every time he jumped, it sounded as if he was breaking wind. And every time that happened, he could hear fits of giggles behind him.

"HAM-ISH, ST..ST..OP.. LAUG-HING

AND TU-RN THE TAP OFF!" he yelled in between gasps of air, jumps, and the *PFFFF, PFFFF, PFFFF* noise of his water-laden shoes.

Hamish had been coming out of the castle's door when he first heard his father's shouts and immediately dropped the box he was carrying. An ominous *SMASH* followed, suggesting he too had added to the number of broken antiques.

Not only was his father drenched, but he was jumping around like a mad man. Hamish ran across to the rusty old tap and twisted it hard to cut the water supply. The hose hit the ground with a *SLAP* and lay motionless, coiled on the cobbles. A final dribble of water ran out of its metal mouth.

Laird Montgomery bent over, panting.

"ID…IDIO…IDIOT HOSE!" he said, struggling to catch his breath. "That's £400 gone on those antiques, just like that!"

He spotted Hamish's crumbled box and added

that to the damages. "Seven hundred pounds...just like that!"

The Laird's shoulders shrank down until they almost disappeared. That was a £799.99 loss this week alone. Three days ago, he had travelled to Crathword to use the library's computer. He had hoped to auction off a silver tray on *eBay*, but having put the zeros in the wrong place accidentally sold the tray for a penny and not the £100 it was worth.

This was all he needed – another loss!

When he finally found his breath, his anger mounted.

"THAT. WHOLE. EPISODE. WAS. NOT. FUNNY!" he growled, doing a time check on his plastic watch, which thankfully had survived the drenching. The gold one had not been so fortunate. Water filled three quarters of the dial, and the hand now appeared to be moving backwards.

"That idiot hose has a mind of its own! Couldn't you see the bother I was in?"

"I wasn't laughing," protested Hamish. "All I did was help. I swear. I came as soon as you shouted and turned the tap off straight away."

"Well, I certainly heard a child sniggering," said his father, shooting him daggers as he wrung out the water from his sleeves and the bottom of his trouser legs. "How do you explain that?"

Hamish couldn't. He had no clue how to explain any of it. It was all utterly unexplainable.

9.

Don't Go Down There!

While Hamish and Gorse had explored every inch of the castle, the old dungeon remained unknown. "YOU MUST NEVER EVER GO

DOWN THERE – EVER," they had been told many times before.

Now, Hamish wasn't the sort of boy who obeyed rules. In fact, he made a habit of flouting them at any given opportunity. But there was something about the old dungeon that unsettled him. Not because of all the banging that could be heard down there at night either. And not even because that's where the castle's prisoners were supposedly once kept.

No, it was wholly down to the horrible dreams he had been having ever since his mother had left.

Yet, when Hamish heard that's where the antiques, or what was left of them, were destined for, he offered his help anyway.

"No, thank you," replied the Laird without a moment's hesitation. "You might slip and hurt yourself. The stairs are very steep. You go and play on your computer."

He reminded his father there was no electricity to do such things.

"Fine, fine, erm, read a book then… Or do some homework. Yes, do some homework. I am sure you have lots of it. Just do something and try not to bother me."

Of course, just like every other night, Hamish had no intention of doing homework.

The banging sound from the dungeon had already begun as it did every evening. But tonight it sounded even louder.

Putting his curling-cornered comic book to the side and looping a tin lantern around his arm, he decided to go and investigate what was happening below.

The north side of the castle was the oldest part and had been built long before the rest. The dungeon, or cellar as the Laird preferred to call it, lay beyond the kitchen and scullery at the very end of the stone corridor, where the low ceiling meant his father was required to bend forward when passing through.

As he approached, the bashing noise grew louder still. There seemed to be a pattern to it. Always, *CREAK, CREAK, BANG, BANNNNG, BANG!* like it was Morse code or something.

Although Laird Montgomery was nowhere in sight, the floor hatch was folded open, revealing a big gaping hole.

It was exactly how it looked in his dream, where he ventured down and disappeared into the darkness, never to make it back out again.

Pushing the lamp inside, its glow lit up a small wooden ladder and the first four steps but no more than that. To get a better look, he decided he would climb down through the hatch but just to the top step and no further. Well, perhaps to the second, but only as far as that.

Hamish quietly lowered himself down with the

lamp still in hand. The temperature immediately dropped, and he wished he had a thicker jumper on. The stairs below the ladder were very steep like his father had said and coiled round tightly. Hamish decided if he just went to, say, the fifth step past the first corner, he would be able to see more.

CREAK, CREAK, BANG, BANNNNG, BANG!

The sound got louder as he made his way a bit further into the dungeon. He had reached the fourth step when Gorse began barking from above the floor hatch. Not a quiet bark either, a deep one, which seemed to sound even louder in the cellar where it echoed off the walls. Perhaps it only felt louder because he knew he shouldn't be down there in the first place.

"Shhhhhh," Hamish hissed upwards.

CREAK, CREAK, BANG, BANNNNG, BANG!

"BARK, BARK, BARK!"

"SHHHHHHHHHHHHHHHH!"

CREAK, CREAK, BANG, BANNNNG, BANG!

"BARK, BARK, BARK!"

Terrified his father would come and see what was going on, Hamish made his way back up. The stairs felt even steeper on his return. His knees brushed his chest as he climbed each step while his heart thudded so hard in his chest that he was sure the pounding could be heard outside his body.

When shadowy ribbons of fire began to flicker from above, he felt relief wash over him. The corridor's torches were now in sight, telling him he was nearing the top. Stretching up to grip the ladder, he felt a tap on his shoulder, so soft that he wondered if it were even a hand.

Hamish jumped, spun round, and almost fell over.

A towering figure loomed over him.

His father.

Laird Montgomery stood completely still, a stony expression fixed to his features. In the illumination of the lamp light, he looked like an old grey statue lit up at night. Meanwhile, the head torch strapped to his forehead shot an interrogating beam into Hamish's face.

"What did I tell you?" began the Laird, who seemed drained of all colour.

"But..."

CREAK, CREAK, BANG, BANNNNG, BANG!

"I told you not to come down here."

"But I was..."

CREAK, CREAK, BANG, BANNNNG, BANG!

"Promise me you won't ever step foot down here again."

"But..."

CREAK, CREAK, BANG, BANNNNG,

BANG!

"PROMISE. ME."

Crossing his fingers behind his back, Hamish nodded his promise and clawed back up through the hatch and into the castle corridor. Gorse lay waiting on the dark stone floor with his nose between his paws.

"Oh, so now you're quiet!" he huffed as he pulled himself up on to his feet.

The deerhound offered a small whine of apology.

It was only as Hamish peered down into the blackness and watched his father retreat round the corner and out of sight that he began to wonder what terrible secret lay inside the dungeon. Something Laird Montgomery surely did not want him to know about.

10.

Sticky Fingers

Wednesdays and Fridays were bread days. That's when Mrs Cook made at least four loaves despite there only being three of them living in the castle, and that number included a dog.

Mrs Cook had been at Drumtipperty Castle for as long as Hamish could remember and probably before that, too. When it came to cooking, she liked to call herself 'inventive' and 'experimental'. In truth, she was awful. Food was under-flavoured, over-peppered, and rubbery from hours of boiling and broiling. Hamish couldn't remember a day even in the height of summer when there wasn't at least two giant metal pots bubbling away on the kitchen's industrial-sized gas stove with a soup, broth, or stew of some kind.

The only thing the housekeeper was very good at was baking bread. Not cakes, not puddings – just bread. The lovely doughy smell would fill every floor of the castle before it was brought out of the oven, cut into wedges the size of doorstops, and smeared with butter an inch thick.

Mrs Cook was a short, round lady, shaped

rather like an apple. By contrast, her frizzy, strawberry blonde hair was cut into a square shape up to her earlobes. She had been both a butcher and a canteen lady previously and had thick, muscular arms from the many hours of pot stirring. Meanwhile, her cheeks were always flushed red from all the steam.

Hamish was unsure what the housekeeper's actual name was. She insisted they call her Mrs Cook because she didn't like her own name. "It's an affa daft name gaen te me fae ma affa daft mither."

Rolling her eyes upwards, she would shake her head at the very thought of it and say "Am affa black affrontit aboot it."

This meant that she wasn't all that happy.

The housekeeper was from a small fishing town in Aberdeenshire, and she spoke in her local dialect. At first, Hamish and Laird Montgomery had found it impossible to understand what she was saying. However, with time, they learned to decipher her unusual word choice, even making sense of it. For the most part, anyway.

That morning, Mrs Cook was already busy in the kitchen despite it not being a Wednesday or a Friday. Today was Tuesday, and Laird Montgomery had two very important guests coming.

"Fit like, loon?" she asked Hamish as he meandered into the kitchen with Gorse by his side. He now knew this to mean, "How are you, boy?"

"Aye, aye," he replied ('hello').

"Yer fither has twa affa special guests coming roon this afterneen," said Mrs Cook, smoothing invisible creases out of her apron with short, fat fingers.

"You're baking cakes for them?" said Hamish, immediately worried for the visitors.

"Aye. Twa of em."

"Two cakes… What kind?"

"Well, the first is an affa fine reid cake."

"A red cake?'

"Aye, a reid cake,"

Mrs Cook picked up her wooden spoon from a bowl that sure enough had the remnants of something very red looking stuck to the sides. This was not the makings of a red velvet cake as one would suspect from a red cake mixture, however. No, this was a tomato soup cake. Two tins of the stuff had been poured into the cake batter earlier.

"A tomato soup cake?" Surely, he had misheard her description.

"Aye, Heinz. Dae ye wintae lick the bowl?"

"Erm, no thanks," he replied, wondering if his father was aware of the unusual cake choice that was to be served to his important guests. "What's the second cake, Mrs Cook?"

"Chocolate."

Like a magician revealing a rabbit, she pulled a checked tea towel off a glass cake stand to unveil what looked like a very normal and very delicious chocolate cake with chocolate icing.

Hamish eyed it suspiciously. "Chocolate?"

"Aye, chocolate."

"Just chocolate? Not chocolate and ham? Not chocolate and cheese? Not chocolate and chopped liver?"

These were all previous combinations that she had made in the past and insisted they try.

"Aye, chocolate. Unfortunately, I dinnae hae muckle ither ingredients in the larder this wik. I need to gae to the shoppee. Anyway, yer fither telt me tae try somethin plainer." Mrs Cook looked around to check no one was listening. "Ye ken, fae folk with plain tastes," she whispered.

If chocolate cake was for those with plain tastes,

then Hamish was such a person.

"Can I please have a slice – a big one – of the chocolate one that is?"

"Aye, loon, ye can but only efter yer fither's guests are awa. I cannae be servin a cake with a whoppin great slice oot o it."

"Oh," said Hamish. Right on cue, his stomach gave a rumble of disappointment. "Can I lick the chocolate bowl then please? Until I get a piece of the actual cake?"

"That bowl is aw' washed I'm afraid, but ye can lick is een." She once again held out the red cake mix bowl.

Before Hamish could decline for a second time, a loud *DINNNNNNNNNNG* rang out from the kitchen timer, signaling that the tomato soup cake was ready. Mrs Cook rubbed her hands together.

"Now, Hamish, if ye thought that the chocolate ein was a winner, wait til ye hae a lookie at this ein. I bet ye've never seen a cake like it afor!"

Hamish very much doubted it either.

But as she pulled her latest creation from the oven, an unfortunate thing happened. Gorse spotted the tail of a small mouse scuttling along the stone slabs by the sink. And, Gorse being Gorse, he had no choice but to pursue the little rodent. It was his job after all – to keep the castle free of all rats and mice.

"AHHHHHHHH," screamed Mrs Cook as the dog almost knocked her off her feet while bolting towards the sink. Then, in what felt like slow motion, the red cake slipped from her oven mitts and landed slap bang on the floor. Meanwhile, the mouse disappeared under a cupboard and out of sight. This allowed the deerhound to make a mad dash back across the kitchen and turn his attention to the smashed cake. Unalarmed by its vibrant colour and unusual flavouring, he plunged his black snout straight into the crumpled sponge.

"MA CAKE! GIT OOT OF MA KITCHIN!" Mrs Cook roared, waving a wooden spoon wildly over her head as Gorse used his lower jaw to shovel the cake down his throat at amazing speed.

Startled by the commotion coming from the other end of the castle, Laird Montgomery appeared at the kitchen door. "What on earth is going on here? Mrs Cook, are you okay?"

"Ma cake, Laird Montgomery. Ma cake, just hae a lookie," she pointed to the floor, where Gorse was finishing up the final crumbs. His long tongue swiped the flag stones for any last morsels.

"Oh goodness, is that the cake for our special visitors?"

"Aye, it wis, Laird Montgomery. Well, ein of them. The chocolate ein across there is still intact."

"And this one?"

"That wis a Heinz tomato soup cake."

"Ah," replied Laird Montgomery, secretly relieved that this particular cake had ended up on the floor and not in the mouths of his visitors.

"Well, I only have two people coming, who will have already eaten lunch, so the chocolate one will be more than adequate. Thank you, Mrs Cook. It looks like quite a showstopper, I must say."

The housekeeper's face quickly changed from an angry red to a shy flush.

"This cake will absolutely help us get the bank loan. I'm sure of it," smiled the Laird. As he left the kitchen, he stopped and stuck his head back in the door to issue a staunch warning to his son.

"Hamish, you and that dog of yours better keep away from that chocolate cake until our visitors have been and gone. We cannot afford another disaster. We just can't."

The cake remained in the kitchen all morning. It stared temptingly out through the glass dome of the cake stand. Hamish considered dipping the very tip of his finger in. "Just the icing, Gorse. What do you say?"

The deerhound made a whining noise.

"I agree, Gorse. Bad idea."

It really wasn't worth getting in trouble for, was it? There were only a few more hours to go before he would be able to get his own slice, guilt-free. He picked up an apple to eat in the meantime.

Laird Montgomery had been preparing for this meeting with the bank for about five days. Every time Hamish walked past his office, he would hear his father reciting various facts and figures. Often the same words but said in a different way. Sometimes he sounded forceful, and other times he sounded pleading. Hamish wasn't sure what voice he had chosen to use today.

With his mind fixed on the chocolate cake, the apple was not proving the distraction Hamish had hoped. Swallowing a second bite, he considered doing some homework. He needed to write a story about a Greek god and practice some percentages before Mrs Stewart returned tomorrow.

With her black rimmed glasses resting on a nose that was as sharp as a compass and hair pulled back into a tight bun that seemed to stretch the skin thinly across her forehead, Mrs Stewart would no doubt tell him that his efforts simply weren't good enough. "You are off to Graceford next year, and the work will be far, far harder," she would reprimand him for the umpteenth time. "They won't tolerate this lack of studiousness."

Having spent a good few minutes thinking about percentages and how to possibly avoid them, Hamish decided to go and take one last glimpse of the chocolate cake before heading to his bedroom.

He could not put his homework off any longer.

Mrs Cook wasn't in the kitchen. Instead, she was tidying the dining room for the visitors. Laird Montgomery would usually have entertained the two men in the drawing room, but this was still out of action with the bird and its continued bowel movements.

Hamish tiptoed into the kitchen and immediately noticed the cake was no longer on the kitchen side where it had been left but on the old wooden table. The glass cover had, however, been lifted off and only a fistful of chocolate crumbs remained on the stand.

"Gorse! The cake!" gasped Hamish, so horrified by its disappearance that he covered his mouth with his hands. "Who…who…who could have possibly eaten it!"

Having been together for the entire time, boy and dog could not point finger or paw at the other as they had done previously when food had gone missing from the kitchen in the past. This time they were each other's alibi.

While Hamish considered what to do next, there was an explosion of giggles in the passageway outside the kitchen. He reeled around. Who had been in the kitchen? Who had eaten the cake that he had managed to resist for all this time? Outraged, he sped along the corridor in the direction of the laughter and discovered a trail of sponge. Gorse hoovered up the little piles, one after another as he went. The crumbs did a loop around the hallway towards the bottom of the north side's stairs, then headed back towards the kitchen, passing the door and into the laundry room.

Nose to the ground, Gorse continued on towards the end of the castle, keen to find more clues. Hamish followed suit. They both stopped dead by the trapdoor down to the old dungeon.

The metal bolts were coated with thick clumps of chocolate icing.

"More chocolate!"

Hamish kneeled down, guarding it from the deerhound who never seemed accepting that chocolate was poisonous to dogs.

The boy touched the icing and pulled it to his nose, giving it a quick sniff to double-check what it was. With Gorse around, you couldn't be too careful.

"Definitely chocolate," said Hamish and licked his fingers. It tasted delicious, and soon he was scooping more off and licking it off his fingers and hands.

"GORSE!"

"YA WEE FURRITT!"

"HAMISH!"

"YER A CLARTY WEE MIDDEN!"

Both boy and dog froze. They didn't need to

turn around to know Laird Montgomery and Mrs Cook were standing behind them, looking very cross.

With chocolate icing smeared around Hamish's mouth and cake crumbs dangling from Gorse's whiskers, this, they imagined, would take some explaining.

11.

The Oldies

For two weeks now, buses had been crunching over Drumtipperty Castle's gravel driveway. Women with grey hair and men with no hair at all climbed down the stairs in trainers that were impossibly white.

"Mind that third step, Maureen," the driver would call, his sunglasses riding his forehead and his enormous stomach resting on the bus's steering wheel. "Bert, have you remembered your medication? Joyce, go easy at the gift shop if they have one, but I wouldn't say no to some of that scrummy Scottish tablet."

Dressed in many different shades of beige, they steadied one another with outstretched arms as if at any moment they were prepared to take a tumble. Thankfully, there had been no falls, but there had been a few near misses.

For as long as Hamish could remember, months would go by without any outside visitors coming to Drumtipperty; coach days were, therefore, met with great excitement.

The big silver bus always arrived early. This was because driver Bob used to race rally cars when he was younger and took no notice of the estate's fifteen miles per hour speed limit, choosing to bounce over the speed bumps at a solid forty-five instead.

Ahead of the bus's arrival, Hamish would take up his usual lookout spot at the rear of the castle and, upon catching sight of it tearing down the tree-lined driveway, would roar, "THE OLDIES ARE HERE!"

This was Gorse's signal to join in the clamour.

The deerhound would commence his sprint of the Grand Lawn, barking madly and running as fast as a greyhound.

Of course, Laird Montgomery was pleased by neither reaction. Such tearaway behaviour was not an image of Drumtipperty he wished to promote, and he, in turn, would storm out of his study to quieten boy and dog down.

"DO NOT, I REPEAT, DO NOT CALL THE LADIES AND GENTLEMEN THAT. THEY ARE OUR VISITORS. THEY ARE OUR SPECIAL GUESTS," he would say in a loud, angry whisper with his fists balled by his side and his face dangerously purple. He would then mutter something about the grey pound.

Hamish didn't understand what this meant, but he knew it had something to do with money. Money was all that his father seemed to care about these days, especially after the visit from the bank didn't go quite as intended.

The ten-year-old was unsure if it had been the lack of chocolate cake or that Lady Foo Foo Archer, having somehow escaped, found her way into the dining room next door. There had been some dropping of bird poo before Mrs Cook managed to usher the bird out and back into the drawing room with her tea towel.

With the dining room door wide open, Gorse made a second unwanted appearance. First, he knocked over two teacups with his wagging tail before helping himself to a tuna and cucumber finger sandwich and a scotch egg. It had been what Laird Montgomery had called a flipping disaster.

In an attempt to rectify matters today, the Laird was travelling down to London to meet with a German bank in the hopes of getting a loan from them instead. He had left very early that morning and would not be returning until the evening. This meant he would not be there to shout at Hamish and Gorse when the morning coach arrived.

As fate would have it, Mrs McCloud, the castle tour guide, wasn't there that day either.

"Please give your father my sincere apologies. I won't be able to come in," she had explained to Hamish who answered the castle's phone, battery-powered to remedy the lack of electricity. "I think I may be coming down with something. My stomach was flip-flopping last night, and I've been very sick."

Although he didn't say it, Hamish thought it could well be the chicken casserole that Mrs Cook served up for lunch the day before. The meat had been suspiciously grey and chewy, and the noisy crow was now missing from the walled garden. Mrs Cook did like to economise when it came to her cooking, and he was beginning to think the big black bird may have ended up in her stew pot.

"You will tell your father, won't you, Hamish?

He knows the drill. He can take my place," said Mrs McCloud before passing a very, loud unpleasant burp – the kind that most certainly tasted of sick.

Hamish agreed and said goodbye. It was only when he hung up that he remembered Laird Montgomery was not in his study but in London meeting the bank. Should he phone his father? He had been given strict instructions not to bother him with any silliness or things of no importance.

Mrs McCloud's absence was certainly not silly, but was it important enough to risk being told off by his father and interrupting yet another important meeting with the bank?

He thought probably not. Plus, what could his dad possibly do from London?

There was nothing else for it; he would have to lead the tour himself.

12.

A Know-it-all Called Ranald

Deciding not to join Gorse with his usual sprint of the lawn as that probably wasn't something somebody who was in charge of a group of adults would do, Hamish went straight to the parking area to greet them.

A group of nineteen grey-haired people stood

in a huddle to the left of the bus, awaiting instruction. Straightening the neck of his top to make himself look a bit tidier, he kept the hood of his jumper up, having not yet brushed his hair that morning.

Hamish cleared his throat to welcome the visitors politely, at least in his mind.

"HELLO, OLD PEOPLE!"

He shouted this greeting, aware that the elderly cannot always hear easily and repeated it for good measure.

"We heard you the first time," someone croaked.

"My name is Hamish Montgomery, and this is my dog Gorse. We will be your castle tour guides this morning."

There was some murmuring.

"Can I ask what age you are?" said a lady at the front with curled, blueish-grey hair.

"Ten. But in case you are wondering, I am small for my age."

There were a few more mumbles from the group.

"So, old ladies and old gentlemen, if you follow Gorse and me, we will give you a quick tour of the castle grounds and gardens first. Then we will show you our awesome castle."

The group began to move off slowly. Those with handbags tucked them under the crook of their arms; others used sticks to help keep their balance as they plodded off the gravel and on to the grass. Three women quickly became detached from the rest of the procession.

"NO STRAGGLERS AT THE BACK, PLEASE!" bellowed Hamish, causing them all to jump and one lady to lose a shoe in the process. Gorse was appointed to bring up the rear after that, gently nudging legs with his snout when they slowed.

Overall, the walk around the grounds was successful. Nobody slipped and fell, and admiring comments were made of the flowers and plants in the walled garden. Thankfully, a few keen gardeners among them were able to answer a number of botanical questions that Hamish had not the foggiest about.

It was the next bit, the inside of the castle, that concerned him most. He really wished he had paid more attention. His father liked nothing more than to ramble on about the history of the various rooms and the bits and pieces in them. At the time, he had found it all very boring, but now this information would have proved extremely valuable.

Having found an old red golf umbrella, Hamish waved it above his head like a tour guide in Venice or Rome might do, instructing the group to follow him. Not only did the brolly make him feel quite important, it helped everyone, who was a half a foot taller than him, to see the direction he was moving in.

The group funnelled through the courtyard and into the reception, taking a right up some stone steps towards the south side of the castle. Hamish climbed halfway up a second stairwell so he could be seen. He cleared his throat.

"Er...so...this is Drumtipperty Castle. It is 874 years old (He remembered that bit.). The castle's tower was built first, and then a few other parts were later added (He remembered that bit, too, mostly because that was where his bedroom was.)."

An elderly man with a thick grey moustache that looked a bit like an uncooked sausage on his lip raised his hand. "The oil painting, just below you in the corner of the stairs, can you please tell us a bit about its origins? How old is it?"

"Hello, sir, thank you for your question."

"Ranald, you can call me Ranald," said the old man.

"Well, Ranald, that painting there is hundreds of years old, quite possibly thousands."

Hamish had never liked the painting. It was a swampy brown colour, and the woman in it had a pinched red nose. "I'm not sure of the precise origins, but if you make a return visit, I shall have the answer!"

There were a few chuckles, and he felt impressed with himself for turning his lack of knowledge into a future ticket sale.

"What else…the castle was attacked a lot in the past. But no enemy was ever successful at getting into Drumtipperty. Not even once!"

"Attacked when? And by whom?" asked Ranald, who was now busy taking pictures of the hallway with a long-lensed camera. Hamish was starting to get annoyed with the old man and all his questions.

He didn't know the answer to that one either.

"There will be a chance to ask questions at the END of the tour – but only if there is time," he said instead and started motioning the group onwards with wide swinging arms as if he were an aircraft marshal directing a plane for take-off. "Now, old people, if you would all like to head along the corridor, I can show you a rare species of bird."

The OAPs began to shuffle off again in the direction of the drawing room.

"Will we be able to see the famous Montgomery Claymore?"

It was Ranald's voice again, calling out from the back.

Hamish thought about ignoring him and

pretending he hadn't heard yet another one of his questions. There was a ninety-nine per cent chance he wouldn't be able to answer it anyway. But this time his ears pricked up, a bit like Gorse's when he heard a strange noise.

"Claymore?" asked Hamish in spite of himself. He didn't know any special claymore existed.

Ranald let go of the camera that was attached to his neck by a thick black strap and ploughed his hand into a plastic carrier bag to produce a pocketbook. Flipping it open, he started to read. Everyone slowed their pace to listen.

"Among the greatest soldiers ever to have lived, Earl Angus Montgomery not only possessed tremendous height and strength, he was also considered a great tactical mastermind. He rode into battle upon a white horse with a claymore that was almost as large as himself. He had only four fingers on his left hand, having lost his middle digit to an archer's arrow when directing a lewd gesture at enemy soldiers. These three traits would become his trademarks."

A white horse, a black sword and a missing finger – exactly like the painting in the drawing room, thought Hamish.

Ranald continued, "The claymore would become the most famous piece of weaponry in Scotland. It was rumoured to have magical powers..."

Magical powers!

"... and to have been cursed..."

Cursed!

"... by a witch."

A witch?!

"According to Scottish legend, in the Earl's old age he came to regret the lives he had taken. Guilt-ridden and seeking peace, he asked the oldest witch in the land to place a spell on the sword. The claymore was lowered into a frozen well in the southernmost tip of Scotland. Then it was placed into a huge fire pit at the northernmost point for the same length of time," read Ranald. "When the sword was pulled from the flames, the curse was complete. The claymore was never to be used by or against another living being. Nor did it ever see battle again."

Why had his father not told him about any of this? wondered Hamish, or perhaps he had, but he hadn't been paying attention at the time. No, he would have remembered such a sword. He was sure of it.

The castle had a few swords on its walls as Scottish castles do although not especially big ones. He decided he would ask the Laird about it when he got back from London. Such a claymore should surely be in the viewing collection. That would attract more visitors to Drumtipperty Castle!

"Ah, what a pity. WE WON'T SEE IT!" shouted out Ranald, having turned the page.

"Why?" asked a heavily perfumed lady to Hamish's left.

"Because the sword was stolen," said the old man, freeing his eyes of the little history book. "It was stolen from the castle over a hundred years ago."

13.

Forever Lost

STOLEN! With a wave of his brolly, Hamish immediately halted the group so that everyone bashed into the person in front of them. He turned and pointed the stick of fabric at Ranald. "What else does the book say?"

The pensioner cleared his throat, pleased he had an audience for a second time that morning. "Three suspects were arrested just outside the village of Crathword. But they were released due to lack of evidence. Experts concluded it was an inside job, involving someone who was close to the Montgomery family."

Hamish and the eighteen elderly listeners gave

a collective gasp.

"What happened to the sword?" piped up a small, bird-like lady with several sets of pearls wrapped around her neck.

"The…the claymore was never found…," replied Ranald, his voice dipping with disappointment. "'Forever lost in history', that's what the book says."

Forever lost! Forever lost! Hamish couldn't believe it. Their castle had once been home to one of Scotland's most famous swords, and it was gone!

How could it have just disappeared into thin air?

With the story now finished, the group continued moving through the gallery, undirected. Eventually they reached the door of the drawing room, where Hamish, who had fallen behind, caught up with them. His mind still fixed on the claymore.

When he turned the door handle, it didn't open like it had done previously. He tried again with no success. Laird Montgomery had no doubt locked it. Perhaps it was for the best. There was no telling what mood Lady Foo Foo Archer was in, and the last thing he needed was the oldies being chased. He had already seen for himself they weren't able to run all that fast having organised a game of rounders during the garden tour. Only Ranald had managed a swinging hit at the ball, which Gorse caught and made off with, and the game was promptly over.

Sneaking a glance at one visitor's wristwatch, he realised there was still another twenty minutes to go before he could take them to the dining room where Mrs Cook would serve some refreshments to end the tour. She was currently in the kitchen preparing her *famous* Nutella and black pudding sausage rolls for them all.

Hamish looked around at the paintings and then the silver from the viewing collection. Nope, he knew nothing about those. As they carried back along the corridor and down the stairs, through the older part of the castle, past winding staircases and arrow slits in the stone walls, he racked his brain for something interesting to say.

It was then he caught sight of the trapdoor leading to the dungeon and grabbed one of the many torches dotted around. Given there was no electricity in Drumtipperty, the Laird made sure they were never far from one at all times.

"Now, if we all stop here," said Hamish coming to a halt. "I will show you the OH-SO DARK DUNGEON of Drumtipperty Castle, full of GHOSTS and GHOOOOOOULS!"

He knelt down and squeezed open the stiff bolts that still felt slightly sticky from the chocolate icing incident, which he had yet to be forgiven for.

"Once the castle dungeon, it was used to imprison Drumtipperty's enemies and remains haunted to this very day. Terrible cries come from deep within," he said, making a few things up and saying it in a scary sounding voice. This, he decided, was far easier than reciting actual historical facts.

At that exact moment, a blood-curdling howl came from below.

"YOWEEEEEEEELLLLLL."

The group fell silent.

"What was that?" asked a woman wearing a long purple cardigan.

"Erm, the ghostly prisoners, I guess," said Hamish, unsure of what the noise was himself.

"OOOOOOOH, HEEEEEELP MEEEEEE," screeched a small, pained voice, followed by a giggle.

"It sounds like a child! Have you got one of

your friends down there?" said the lady with the blue hair.

"Yes, are you playing some kind of trick on us?" said another woman suspiciously.

"No… No, I'm not," stuttered Hamish. "I think its maybe the old boiler… That's what my dad says… But I actually don't know why it's making that strange noise."

"If that's a boiler, I'm the King of Scotland!" said Ranald, angrily snatching away the torch that Hamish was shining in. "I'm going down there to see what's what!"

It was at this point that Hamish realised that Ranald was the only man among a group of women he seemed to be trying to impress.

"Ranald, be careful!"

"Ranald, you are very brave!"

"Ranald, we will wait for you," were among the concerned cries as he lowered himself down through the hatch.

It took Ranald several minutes to get himself and his dodgy hip through the hatch. This helped use up some more time. Everyone was too anxious to ask questions about the castle or its history, and for that, Hamish was grateful. The women murmured among themselves when they thought he would be back and how he was doing a very dangerous but courageous thing.

The old man was gone for some time before eventually returning. He reappeared through the hatch with his grey moustache covered in white cobwebs and his face smeared with oily grime. The group of women crowded around him, patting his back and squeezing his arm as they helped him out of the black hole.

"Ranald, are you ok?"

"Could you see anything down there?"

"Was there a child?"

"Ranald, what's wrong? You look like you've seen a ghost," asked the lady in the long cardigan.

For once, Ranald remained quiet and did not utter another word for the rest of the tour.

14.

Big, Big, Big Trouble

Laird Montgomery received a phone call from the tour company when he returned home from London. Several complaints had been made about the age of the castle guide, "Who at ten years old surely did not qualify for such a role. Nor should a large dog for that matter."

The lady's voice was uncompromising. "With this in mind, the contract with Silver Life Tours and Drumtipperty Estate will be terminated with immediate effect."

This meant that the oldies were no longer coming to the castle.

This also meant Laird Montgomery was not in the least bit happy.

"I was only trying to help," Hamish pleaded when he was told to go straight to his room with only a sandwich for his supper. "I thought I'd better not bother you while you were in London. Like you told me not to."

"Hamish, telling me that Mrs McCloud is not here to do her job is completely different to you telling me that Gorse has eaten his own sick or that you've broken your own record for stuffing as many pieces of shortbread in your mouth as you can. I told you not to bother me with silly things like that. This, however, was very, very important!"

Hamish didn't think he had ever seen his father this angry before.

"The German bank in London didn't give us the loan, and now we have lost the contract with the tour company. Don't you understand we desperately needed that money!"

"But…I," Hamish started again.

"Enough, I don't want to hear it, not this time. NOW, GO TO YOUR BED. I'm tired. I have been travelling all day. I've really had enough for one evening."

Hamish walked out of the kitchen with his head held so low his chin pressed against the neck of his sweatshirt.

"Aye, the bairn's a tumshie, nae doot," said Mrs Cook as she handed over a towering sandwich, constructed of three giant slices of bread and stuffed full of melted cheese. A mug was held out, too, concealing hot chocolate, his favourite drink. “But his hert’s in the right place.”

Hamish felt angry with himself. If only he had known more about the castle, the tour wouldn’t have been such a disaster, and the old people would probably be coming back.

With his oil lantern hooped over his left arm, his hot chocolate in one hand and sandwich in the other, he set off in the direction of his bedroom, wondering how he could possibly make things better.

Think! Come on, think, he demanded of himself as Gorse shadowed behind.

He wasn’t halfway down the torch-lit corridor when he had a brainwave. Actually, it was his second one. The first he had already discounted because he had a niggling suspicion that the

Guinness Book of World Records did not pay record holders or those attempting them. Getting five fingers of shortbread in his mouth at one time, possibly a sixth, was no mean feat, but unless there was some prize money or winnings at the end of it, it would be a pointless endeavour.

His second idea required no biscuit eating. But it did require studying. In fact, he could hardly believe he was even considering it. But desperate times call for desperate measures as the saying went, and for his plan to work, he would have to start by learning all about the castle and its history. Once he had collected enough information and memorised it all, or maybe written it down on some cue cards, he could become Drumtipperty's official tour guide. He would then work for free. To begin with, anyway.

Of course, this self-appointed role depended on the castle getting another contract with some new old people. But surely that wouldn't be too hard. An ageing population, that's what the news said. Wasn't the country being overrun by them all?

Deciding to seek out some information on Drumtipperty's history, he headed to the library, which was tucked away in a tiny, draughty room in the old wing of the castle at the opposite end of the corridor to the dungeon. It wasn't much of one. In fact, it wasn't all that bigger than a large cupboard. There were twelve books shelves in total, stretching from the floor up as far as the ceiling. The first eleven shelves were wonky and tipped diagonally downwards, so everything was disorderly. The books themselves were dark green or brown in colour – all old and uninteresting in appearance. Except one.

The very top shelf was as straight as a ruler and on it sat a single book. Unlike the rest, this one was red with shiny gold buckles on each of its four corners. He felt instantly drawn to it.

Now, how was he going to reach it? There wasn't a ladder in sight, so he began taking books from the lower shelves to make a step. He placed one on top of the other and made a tall pile. Then he realised it was far too high for him to get his foot on to it in the first place without knocking it down.

Next, he built several piles of books. The second was higher than the first, and the third was higher than the second and so on. He hoped to step from one up onto the next, almost like a ladder. That didn't work either because by his fourth pile, the tower of books had become dangerously wobbly and threatened to topple over.

As a last resort, he tried to knock the red book off the shelf by throwing one of the brown books at it. The brown book got stuck up there, too.

“This is never going to work, Gorse!”

Feeling defeated, Hamish plonked himself on the cold stone ground next to his dog. After spending a good few minutes feeling sorry for himself for a second time that evening, he decided he’d better return the books to their rightful place on the shelves.

But just as he was preparing to push himself up, a gust of cold air blasted into the room, and with a *THUD* the red book now lay on the ground in front of him.

15.

The Montgomery Family Archive

Hamish stared at the book for a full minute, unsure if a draught had blown in from under the old crooked door, where there was a six-inch gap between it and the floor. Or had it been something else?

Whatever it was or had been, he picked the book up, feeling grateful.

"C'mon, Gorse." Hamish decided to take it back to his bedroom and read it there. There was a good chance his father would come and check on him, and he really didn't want to be grounded any more than he already was. Although what restrictions could actually be imposed, he was uncertain. With no electricity for TVs, games consoles or tablets, punishments were in short supply.

Back in his bedroom, he placed the lamp and the hot chocolate on his rickety wooden bedside table and piled up a small mountain of pillows. Taking a seat on his bed, he began eating his sandwich one-handed, using the other to push the pages of the book open. Gorse jumped up to join him, eyeing the cheesy bread wishfully.

At first glance, the book was disappointing. The beginning was full of blank pages. It seemed to start at the back instead. Yet, the very last pages were so tatty and discoloured, they were impossible to read. As he flipped further through the book from back to front, the paper got a bit less old, and he could just about identify some small drawings. What the pictures were actually of, he wasn't sure until two pages later, where he discovered the face of an old man. Next to the picture, he could just about make out an *A*, and then a *G*, and an *O*. Actually, no, it was a *U,* then an S. *Angus*! It must be a drawing of his ancestor, Angus Montgomery! Underneath the name was two sets of dates, but the numbers were illegible.

This picture of the Earl was very different to the one in the drawing room. In fact, if it weren't for his name next to it and a missing finger, Hamish was not sure he would have believed it was him. Just as Hamish had requested that Gorse be in his portrait, Angus had presumably chosen his closest comrade, his horse.

In this particular drawing, his ancestor looked very old. He had lost almost all of his hair, and his bushy beard was reduced to no more than a few sparse hairs sprouting from a long chin that came to a sharp point. Meanwhile, his body seemed to have shrunk. His chest, shoulders, and arms had lost their vast width and depth, and he appeared a bit crumpled, like when air is sucked out of a plastic bottle.

Unlike the rest of him, Angus's hands had maintained their great size. Without the claymore clutched in them, they resembled two big shovels. Hamish wondered where the sword was. It had not yet been stolen from the castle, after all.

Taking a break, the boy drained his mug in one. With a line of cocoa now coating his top lip, he opened the book up again, only to find his own face staring back at him – minus the chocolate moustache.

Hamish Alexander Montgomery

Born 19/10/2010

His own picture and date of birth confirmed that this was the Montgomery family archive – something he had not held or seen before. When he had been drawn previously, the book was placed on a large wooden easel and immediately whisked away by his father wearing white gloves.

"The pages are much too delicate for you to handle," he had been told. "They are so old they may well crumble in your hands."

Hamish wondered what the Laird would say if he saw him handling the book now. With that thought, he put the rest of his melted cheese sandwich down and wiped his hands back and forth along his patchwork bedcover a couple of times to clean them up a bit. This provided Gorse with the opportunity he had been waiting for, and the unguarded cheesy bread was demolished in two seconds flat.

Although the portrait was dated as his birthday, he appeared glum. Then he remembered why.

"I'm afraid we are having to tighten our belts again," Laird Montgomery had said while presenting him with a small rattling box of

Maltesers instead of the Nintendo Switch that he had requested. If that hadn't been bad enough, Mrs Cook had cut him an extra large slice of her special Irn-Bru and square sausage flavoured birthday cake, which had actual chunks of grey grisly meat sandwiched in between luminous layers of orange sponge.

Even after such terribleness, he had then been requested to sit as still as a statue for two hours straight while his portrait was redrawn, as it would be every year, in order to keep the archive up to date. All in all, it had been a miserable birthday, and it was reflected in the grimace of his inked face.

"This is the way it has been done for hundreds and hundreds of years, and it shall continue to be done this way," the Laird maintained when his son suggested there must be a more twenty-first century way of keeping a record of castle residents, past and present. "This is the Montgomery book, not Facebook!"

When Hamish turned the page, he saw that Laird Montgomery was not smiling in his own picture either. Rather, his mouth sloped downwards at the corners into a thin, downturned moon. He wondered if his father had been any happier in past portraits when Mrs Montgomery was still around. There was no evidence of his mother in the book. The neighbouring page was blank. Studying the paper more closely, Hamish could see something had been scrubbed out and that a drawing of some form had been there previously. If he held the page up against the lantern light, he could almost make out a faint outline. There was a small nose and big eyes, like his. Unlike the other women in the book, who seemed to have their hair in dark, tight ringlets, hers looked much lighter and fell in long, soft curls.

There was not one photo of his mother in the house. Laird Montgomery had removed every single frame after she left, even if she wasn't in the picture herself. It was like any memory of their past lives with her was just too painful.

Rather than upsetting his father, he had asked Mrs Cook for more information.

"Aye, she's a affa bonny quine. There's nae doot aboot it. Maybe oor bonnie for her ane gweed. Affa easy led. She thought only o' herself and er ain coorse ways. She brought yer fither a great deal of hurt… Ken in a lot of ways I blame maself."

"Why would you blame yourself?" Hamish had asked, wondering whether he could blame Mrs Cook, too. He was always looking for someone to blame for his mother's disappearance.

"Well, it was ma' brother..." Mrs Cook never finished her sentence. "I'll tell ye fin yer auler, loon."

He hadn't heard or asked anymore since.

While he pushed her out of his thoughts through the day, at night he would find himself dreaming about her. Sometimes they were good dreams, where she was back at the castle and they were laughing over one of his jokes or she was reading to him, even though he was a good reader himself. He liked to hear her voice say the words aloud. She always kissed his forehead goodnight to which he protested, "Mum, no, get off!" knowing they would repeat the ritual the next night, too.

But there was also a bad dream, one that haunted him for days after. In it, he was crouched outside the trapdoor. He slid the bolts open and slipped inside to search for her. No sooner had he climbed in than—*BANG!* The trapdoor thudded shut, leaving him to pound his fists desperately to be let out. It was always at that point that he woke.

And the nightly *CREAK, CREAK, BANG, BANG, BANG* would be rising up from the old dungeon and into his bedroom.

Hamish shuddered. He missed his mum far more than he let himself admit. He spent all his time trying not to think about her, so he wouldn't get himself upset. What was the point? That wouldn't bring her back, would it? He guessed his father had done the same.

The thought of her now made his eyes feel hot and wet and his heart hurt. He squeezed his eyelids shut. But it was too late. At least three tears rolled down his cheek, splashing on to the blank page where his mother's drawing should have been, causing a blotch to appear. It grew to the size of a two pence coin.

Through the wet paper, feature by feature, a different face began to emerge. A boy, who looked a bit like himself, but younger. Hamish peeled back the book's pages to identify the mystery face. Yes, the boy was five, according to the description next to him.

Struan Montgomery

Born 24/11/1898

Death (by misadventure) 20/05/1904

Using the pictures and dates of people before and after, Hamish worked out Struan was his father's grandfather's youngest brother.

Misadventure? What did that mean? The opposite of adventure? Boredom? Surely Struan hadn't died of actual boredom? Although, there had been plenty of times that Hamish felt he may die of that himself, especially when it was raining and there wasn't a single watt of electricity in the castle to do anything.

Once again, the ten-year-old cast his mind

back to the times he had seen a small shadow darting around the castle, the child's laughter, and the stolen chocolate cake.

"What do you think, Gorse?"

Having finally collected the remaining toast crumbs hidden in the creases of the bedcover, the sprawling deerhound offered no comment.

Hamish took another long, hard look at the boy's drawing.

"I don't know about you, Gorse, but I'm starting to think Struan Montgomery may be the castle ghost or something..."

And with those words, the oil lamp on his bedside table blew out, plunging the room into darkness.

16.

A Ghostly Visitor

Anyone else may well have panicked when everything went black unexpectedly. But if you live in an old Scottish castle, you can't scare easy. You just can't.

Hamish had long been used to the dark. In fact, he had the layout of his bedroom and its entire contents committed to memory. Reaching down, he felt for the wooden box that he kept underneath his bed. Inside, there was a random collection of things. This included a compass (he wasn't sure why as he hated maths), a penknife, and a triple prize-winning conker. Next, his hands identified an old perfume bottle of his mother's (this had the tiniest amount of liquid remaining at the bottom, but just enough to smell), a kilt pin, a silver medal from a running race at Crathword village fete (he had been the youngest by far, a fact he proudly remembered), and… And… The matches. Finally!

SWWWHHHH.

The flame lit a circle of light, enough to see that a boy was sitting cross-legged in front of him. At first, Hamish thought he was staring at his own reflection. Then he remembered he didn't have a mirror in his bedroom. Nor was he wearing strange, puffy shorts with long socks and old-fashioned lace-up shoes either. Or a hat for that matter.

When he opened his mouth to yell, the boy did the same, blowing out the match with a single puff as if it were a birthday candle. The room once again went black.

Unsure what to do next, but deciding a scream was unnecessary given the size of the child, Hamish spoke into the darkness. "Hello? HELLO? HE-LLLLLL-OOO?"

There was the sound of another match being lit. A small halo of light appeared, this time around the little boy.

"I didn't want you to burn your fingers," the child said quietly.

"Oh," said Hamish. "Won't you burn yours?"

The orange flame stayed fixed to the very tip of the boy's match, however, and did not move.

The boy shook his head and giggled.

There it was! That laugh! Hamish recognised it

instantly. It was the one he heard in the corridor when the chocolate cake mysteriously disappeared and the one that was in the cellar during the castle tour.

The boy's laugh was not the only familiar thing about him. Hamish had seen him somewhere before, too.

The Montgomery family archive he had just been looking through, of course! The boy was the person who appeared through the page. It was the same face.

"You're Struan Montgomery, aren't you?"

The boy nodded, pleased he had been identified.

"So if you are Struan, that means you're...dead?"

The boy nodded again, this time more slowly, as if considering his answer.

Hamish had never seen anyone dead before. He

leaned forward to have a closer look. Although Struan had a faint cut on one side of his head, he didn't look especially dead. His skin was pale but not considerably. The Scottish word peely-wally best summed up his pasty pallor.

"If you are dead, does that make you...a ghost?"

"Well, technically yes," said Struan, finally breaking his silence. "But I'm only a ghost when I'm down here – on earth. Otherwise, I am a dead boy up there." He pointed his finger upwards.

"Aren't they one and the same thing?"

"No, they are quite different," said the ghost-slash-dead boy. "Anyway, I hope I didn't scare you."

"No, you didn't," Hamish replied a bit too quickly. "I'm not scared of a five-year-old boy – ghost or no ghost."

In truth, he was a little scared, but he wasn't

going to tell someone who was half his age that. He looked over at Gorse, who was now flat-out sleeping. Some guard dog he was.

Hamish wondered whether it was impolite to ask how a ghost died, but he decided to anyway.

"Tree climbing," replied the dead boy.

"Tree climbing!" Hamish repeated, astonished. Dead from tree climbing! Tree climbing! Hamish had likely climbed thousands of trees in his life, probably more. He had hoped there was another sixty years of climbing trees left in him. Yet with this revelation, the future of his favourite pastime now felt like it was in jeopardy.

"Was it the big, old oak that did it? That tree is impossible to climb!"

Struan nodded. "I got to the eleventh branch, but it broke and..." the five-year-old motioned to his pale body, "this happened."

Hamish had only ever got as far as the ninth

branch, but he had fallen and twisted his ankle so badly he had limped home using Gorse as a crutch. He decided Struan's accident was as good a warning as any that he shouldn't attempt that particular climb again.

"If you don't mind me asking, why are you here, Struan? At Drumtipperty, I mean?"

"Oh, I've been busy haunting you all."

"Have you?" said Hamish, unable to disguise his surprise. True, a few strange things had happened here and there, but he hadn't been especially scared. And weren't ghosts meant to scare you silly?

"You have to start with small stuff," Struan shrugged as if reading his mind. "You build up the spookiness. You can't just go in and start terrifying people from the off. That's the rules."

"The rules of what exactly?"

"The rules of being a ghost. There is a

looooooooong list of them. I have to study them all. Drumtipperty is my first ever haunting."

Four dust-covered books materialised in Struan's pale hands. At the top of the stack were two white ones called *The Ghost Guidance Handbook Volume I* and *II.* Underneath was a pale grey book called *Going Ghosting,* and below that was a black and white one called *BOO: A Guide to Haunting Loved Ones.*

How awful, thought Hamish. There really was no escaping schoolwork, even when dead and a ghost.

The books disappeared from the little boy's hands as quickly as they appeared. Struan got up and dusted himself off and began to pace the small patch of available floor space, which meant walking one step forward, turning, and walking one step back.

"You see, for years, us ghosts have been getting

a really bad rap. Everyone has been thinking we are these horrible things, and as a result, our membership went down. No one was signing up. Everyone passing through just wanted an easy death—to relax, catch up with family, maybe travel—all that kind of stuff." Struan stopped to shrug before setting off on his one-step pace again. "So there has been a big shake-up from the top of the ghosting world. The hauntings are continuing, the grassroots don't want to give that up, but we are having a big image overhaul. To encourage future recruits, we are now permitted to help people. Once we've had some fun frightening them first. Hahahaha!"

Hamish frowned. "I'm sorry, Struan, but you really haven't scared us all that much. You've only gotten me in trouble."

"Oh," said the ghost boy, his voice heavy with disappointment. "How so?"

"The broken antiques, the old people, the chocolate cake." The ten-year-old ticked them off his fingers one by one.

Still holding the match, Struan lowered himself on to a corner of the bed, looking like the wind had been knocked out of him. "I didn't mean for that to happen," he said with his head hung low. "I was only trying to help the Laird after he smashed the first lot of antiques. I know my levitation skills aren't up to much. Not yet, anyway. And with the old people… I had fun scaring them. It's in my ghosting genes, I suppose. But I also thought I was helping. I was adding a bit of atmosphere to your story."

Hamish raised an eyebrow. "And the chocolate cake?"

"Erm, I just really love cake. I'm sorry."

"You should be!" scolded the living boy. "You didn't leave a single slice. It was the only nice thing

Mrs Cook has made all year, aside from bread, and you ate the whole thing! All you are is a naughty, cake-thieving five-year-old, and I don't even think you can do anything ghostly!"

"Wait, no! I can do *this*."

It happened in a nanosecond. The room went dark again, and then Struan and his match light appeared in the opposite corner of the bedroom by the desk.

"Right, well… fine, that is pretty cool," Hamish confessed.

"I can also do *this*."

The younger boy performed an un-ghostly cartwheel in the small nook of space that wasn't taken up by furniture. The spinning match light made him look like a Catherine wheel and appear a serious fire hazard at the same time.

"Well, I can do stuff, too," said Hamish, demonstrating his own gymnastics with a wobbly crab walkover. "But you still haven't told me why you're here. Haven't you got anything better to do than haunt us?"

While Hamish almost smashed the mug off his bedside table with a flailing foot, Struan did his magical reappearing thing and caught it just in time. "Like I said, I've come to help you, not just scare you."

"Help, how?"

"I'm here to deliver some very important information that will help save Drumtipperty. We're worried that if you keep on as you are, you may end up losing the castle."

"Who's 'we' exactly?"

"The Montgomerys. There was a big family meeting," Struan gestured toward the ceiling for a second time, "you know, *up there*. Everyone chose me to come down and help."

"You?" exclaimed Hamish in disbelief. "Out of

874 years of Montgomerys, they picked *you*?"

"Well, a lot of them are pretty old. They couldn't face the long journey... And not sleeping in their own beds—"

"But really, a little five-year-old!" interrupted Hamish. "Couldn't they have sent Earl Angus? They should have really sent *him*, if anyone! Him and his sword!"

Struan's white complexion tinged red with anger. "Earl Angus was eighty-three when he died, so he's really old as a ghost, too! Besides, they sent me *because of the sword*. And I bet if I lived until I was ten, I would be far taller than you!"

Hamish considered wrestling Struan to the floor, but he didn't know if it was possible to fight a ghost. Would he just fall straight through him? Or worse, did Struan have some ghostly superpower strength that would knock him out flat? He decided not to find out.

"So what information do you have to tell me?" he asked instead, his arms folded.

"Oh, so now you want to hear from the little five-year-old? Now you want to know?"

"Okay then, don't tell me!"

"Okay, I'll tell you," Struan said, quickly relenting. The whole point of his assignment was to pass on the information. Scaring aside, he couldn't very well go back up without having at least accomplished that part. He would never be sent on another ghosting again.

It was time he completed his mission. Yes, it was time he spoke the truth.

The boy-ghost removed his cap as he began to give his testimony. "I was sent down here because I was there the night the claymore was taken. I saw it all, Hamish."

17.

A Witness at the Scene of the Crime

"I saw the three burglars disappear into the dungeon with the sword," said Struan, dropping yet another bombshell of which there had been many that evening. "They kept complaining it was getting heavier and heavier. They never came back out."

Hamish felt his jaw fall open. "But how is that possible? They were captured near Crathword. That's what the books say—or at least Ranald's one did."

Struan began to swear on his life but stopped. Being dead, such an oath wasn't worth much. So instead he said, "They never came back out. I promise. I stayed up all night and into the morning, too, waiting for them."

Hamish thought for a while. "But why didn't you tell anyone what happened?"

"I *did* try to tell them all!" exclaimed Struan, clearly still upset by the matter. "But no one would listen. Everyone was in such a panic that the sword was missing, they didn't take any notice of a five-year-old. They thought I was making it up."

"And not one other person woke up that night?"

"No. I got up because my stomach was rumbling. I crept downstairs in my pyjamas to sneak some food from the kitchen, and that's when I saw them going down into the dungeon. Our cook, Mrs Burwick, made pheasant stew for dinner that night, and I refused to eat it, so I was sent to bed without any dinner. Every day I fed the birds in the garden. I wasn't going to eat one."

Between Struan's fondness for cake and birds,

Hamish was starting to think that he and this dead boy might be more alike than he first thought. Then he remembered the blue pheasant that was residing in the drawing room.

"Lady Foo Foo Archer..."

"I brought her with me," said Struan with a cheeky grin. "She's a Montgomery too."

"You did? She is?"

"Yes! Just like Gorse is! Once you have your picture in the family archive that means you're a Montgomery for life – for eternity actually. You do know Lady Foo Foo Archer is on the cover?"

So Mr Guillemot was right, thought Hamish. "But why did you bring her here in the first place? What exactly is the point of her being here?"

"Because she is part of this story, too. Lady Foo Foo Archer is here to help."

"Hmm," said Hamish, unconvinced. The blue bird hadn't exactly done much aside from eat and go to the toilet. "In that case, can you please ask her to start helping soon, Struan?"

The castle's financial situation was worsening by the day. Only yesterday, another bill with **FINAL WARNING** stamped across in red was delivered and put straight into the *Can't-Afford-It* pile in his father's study. Come to think of it, all the bills were placed in that stack. The *Can-Afford-It* pile consisted only of the piece of paper with those words written on it.

"Right, I better be off," said Struan, leaning over the bed and patting a snoring Gorse, goodbye with his one free hand.

"What? You are leaving? Will you be back tomorrow?"

Although he wouldn't admit it, Hamish was quite enjoying the company. Even with the five-year age gap.

"No, I won't. I have to go back now. You have

to figure the rest out yourself. The Ghosting Code of Conduct only lets me help you so far, and I've already been away far longer than I should have. My family will be missing me now."

Hamish suddenly had a thought.

"Struan, you haven't seen my mum when you were up there? I don't know if you know, but she went missing five years ago. We haven't heard from her since. I was starting to wonder if something may have happened to her. I can't think why she wouldn't have been in touch otherwise."

"What does she look like? There are a lot of us."

Hamish pulled the Montgomery archive off his bed and turned to the page next to his father's.

"You can't see too much anymore, just an outline really."

The match lit up the page so the faint pencil lines of his mother almost came to life.

"No," he replied after some thought. "She's

very pretty, isn't she? I would have remembered her. She doesn't look like a Montgomery either."

Hamish felt relief wash over him. His mother was still alive. "Does my father know about you? Has he met you?"

Struan shook his head again. "No, and it's probably best to keep this between us. Grown-ups just don't believe in stuff like ghosts. I'm not sure their brains have the capacity."

Hamish had to agree. His father didn't seem to think anything especially strange was happening at the castle. He just thought it was all down to his own son misbehaving.

"Right, I've really got to get going now, but if I am to give you one last piece of advice, it is to tell you that the Montgomery archive will help you."

"But why is that red book so important? It's so old, I can barely read it."

The match that Struan was holding was getting

dimmer.

"Because that's where 874 years of our family history lies. That's where more answers are hidden."

Hamish wasn't sure if it was the dark room and his eyesight straining, but Struan seemed to be getting smaller now, too. The young boy's body was beginning to shrink. Soon, he was no bigger than a fairy, albeit one dressed in long socks and a funny cap.

"Just remember, with weakness sometimes comes strength. Remember how you found me, Hamish," a tiny voice said from the corner of the room.

Struan and his pinprick of match light disappeared completely then.

18.

Cousin Alice

When Hamish woke the next morning with Gorse snoring loudly beside him, he wondered if had dreamt the entire thing.

But then he saw two burnt out matches lying

on the stone floor below him, which made him think maybe, just maybe, Struan had been there. And maybe, just maybe, the Montgomery Claymore wasn't lost forever.

For the next three days, Hamish agonised about what to do. He couldn't think of anything else, certainly not schoolwork. Thoughts of the claymore circled his head. When he was unable to give one correct answer on his Ancient Greece project, he was ordered to do extra homework on top of what he already had.

Hamish's mind was much too busy to be concerned about that, though. Tomorrow, Alice was due to arrive at Drumtipperty for her annual summer holiday.

Cousin Alice wasn't like many girls in terms of her likes and dislikes. Although Hamish knew very few to make that comparison, really only Mrs Cook, Ms Stewart and Mrs McCloud. But blue was her favourite colour, and she disliked pink AND purple. She hated anything sparkly and with unicorns. When Alice drew, she sketched pictures of rockets, spaceships, and aliens – very ugly aliens with lots of eyeball sockets bursting out of their spotty, pus-oozing bodies. She was even better at drawing F1 racing cars and could compose a perfect McLaren 720S from memory.

Alice drew with her left hand. She didn't do a single thing with her right one, not even hold a fork. Her right arm tucked inwards and bent at the wrist into a loose fist shape. Both hand and arm hung by her side with no real use or purpose.

The last time Alice had visited Drumtipperty, Hamish decided to ask her what had happened. It was autumn. The trees had begun to shed their rusty-coloured leaves. They were outside throwing pebbles into the small stone birdbath in the castle's walled garden. Alice was winning as usual.

"It's cerebral palsy," she had told him matter-of-factly. "I was born with it. But some people have it much worse."

Alice had the kind which only affected one side of her body a bit, and her arm mostly, not her leg. Kids could still be cruel, though, making jokes and jibes, but she tried to ignore it if she could.

"Instead, I make sure I do the absolute best I can at everything I do, even the things I feel I'm not very good at," she had told him as she fired another pebble into the birdbath with her other arm, making it twelve stones to his nine. The silver charm bracelet on her left wrist made a jangling noise with every throw.

His cousin was someone to confide in, at least about the sword. He hadn't yet decided whether he would tell her about Struan. In the end he did.

"I believe you," she said, sweeping her brown fringe from her eyes as they stood exactly fifteen metres from the birdbath, which had previously been measured and marked with a moss-covered rock. "I know for a fact ghosts are real. My grandma used to have one in her old cottage called Deidre who liked to drink whisky and gamble. I never saw her, but my grandma told me all about her."

Hamish was relieved Alice was so accepting of Struan. It would have been impossible to show her actual evidence that he existed otherwise. A burnt-out match wasn't exactly proof. And Gorse didn't make much of a witness either.

To be sure no one overhead their conversation, the cousins headed to the walled garden, which was enclosed with very tall red brick walls and a heavy green wooden door, complete with rusty bolt. Inside, there were lots of plants, flowers, and hedge rows with sandy-coloured pathways running in between.

For over 200 years, fruit and vegetables had

been grown there. The garden provided produce for the castle's occupants long before supermarkets existed. Even back then, the Montgomerys were able to grow what were considered very exotic fruits of the time, like grapes, figs and peaches. This was thanks to a special outdoor heating system in the garden. A group of boilers would heat the south wall, feeding warmth into the greenhouses.

Mrs Cook still relied on the walled garden. Unable to get to the shops that often and with the supermarket refusing to do home delivery because of the endless, twisty-turny roads to Drumtipperty, she got much of the kitchen's vegetables and herbs from there, which she tended to and grew. Meanwhile, all the meat and eggs were collected from the neighbouring farm.

"So the sword could still be in the castle?" asked Alice as they began walking the garden path, which crunched underfoot.

“Yes, or at least somewhere around about it,” replied Hamish. “Struan saw the burglars disappear into the dungeon with the claymore, and they never came back out. When they were caught just outside of Crathword, it was without the sword. The claymore was never found.”

“So we have to figure how they somehow managed to get out of the castle through the old dungeon. There’s got to be another way to get out down there!”

Hamish agreed. “We need to search the dungeon, don’t we?”

“Yes, but first we need some more clues. We should have a good study of that Montgomery book you have.”

Hamish didn’t much like the word study, but if it helped find the sword, it would be more than worth it. Struan had said there was more information in the book, so it really was their best starting point.

They filed out of the garden having completed five loops of the pathways, followed by ten stone throws, which Alice won. Hamish shut the garden door firmly behind them. Mrs Cook would go berserk if he let the rabbits in. Not one plant had been spared from their nibbles the last time he had failed to bolt the door properly.

Before they were able to take a look at the book, Hamish first needed to feed Lady Foo Foo Archer. That was one of his responsibilities along with keeping the drawing room as poo-free as possible and providing weekly progress reports.

Mr Guillemot had attached an electronic tracking device into the bird's foot with the use of a specialist dart gun. This was to monitor her daily habits for research purposes. Laird Montgomery was convinced a secret camera had been installed in the black plastic, too. It hadn't. But this didn't stop the castle owner from ranting, "I will not be spied on in my own home!" every time he passed through the gallery and by the doors of the drawing room.

Mr Guillemot had not yet returned to Drumtipperty. His car was in the garage undergoing some major repairs.

"It is almost fixed, thank you. It just needs a new engine," the ornithologist explained when they last spoke on the phone. "I shall hopefully be paying you all a visit very soon."

As the bird's primary caregiver, the key to the drawing room was now kept in Hamish's own pocket rather than his father's. Although there were no precious antiques inside, the Laird still insisted the door was kept locked. A fierce, exotic bird residing in the drawing room was bad, but a fierce, exotic bird loose in the castle, perhaps able to find its way into the Green Room – the Laird's bedroom in the middle of the night – was far, far worse.

"This is us," said Hamish, halting outside the drawing room. With Struan no longer lodging, the door opened as it should with a simple turn of the key.

Inside the room, it was all quiet. This meant Lady Foo Foo Archer was probably snoozing in the far corner by one of the hard, low sofas, a favoured spot of hers when the sun was shining through the tall, thin windows.

Perfect, he thought. He could dump the bread and be gone before she woke up, saw the measly portion of food, and found her temper.

The blue bird had gotten quite fat from all the castle's leftover bread. Having deviated from Mr Guillemot's feeding chart, Hamish was to blame for the weight gain. With the bird officer's visit now looming, he had no choice but to reduce portion sizes. Considerably.

Little and often was not a concept that pleased Lady Foo Foo Archer, however. Particularly when a bowl and not the regular bucket of bread she had become accustomed to was presented at the foot of the fireplace.

The last two times he had dared curb her portions, there had been a blood-curdling shriek, then a mid-air poo attack. Fortunately, the hood of his jumper had protected him from much of the downpour.

As he placed the bowl at the fireplace and silently slid his fingers out from underneath in the hope that she wouldn't be alerted to his whereabouts, he felt something hard in his mouth and presumed he had a lost a tooth. His left back molar had been wobbly for some time now, and he spent much of his day poking the tip of his tongue against it. So the last thing he expected to pull from his mouth was a small muddy stone.

"What's that?"

Alice peered over his shoulder to see what he was holding between his thumb and forefinger, but before he could answer, she shouted, "Look! Look at the painting, Hamish!"

At first, he didn't see what his cousin was seeing. Earl Angus was still sitting on his white horse with sword in hand. Nothing unusual there. The tree was there, too, although admittedly it seemed to have grown much taller and a blue bird that looked rather like Lady Foo Foo Archer was now perched in one of its branches. It was further into the painting's background that his cousin was referring to – so far away that the three dark shapes were almost disappearing into the horizon.

Somehow, Hamish, Alice and Gorse were all in the painting.

19.

The Curse

Back in his bedroom, Hamish disappeared under his bed to dig out the archive, sweeping off a bit of dried cheese that had stuck to the cover.

Alice sat on the patchwork bedcover with her

knees pulled up to her chest. "That was really weird with the painting. It really spooked me. Didn't it freak you out?"

Hamish gave a shrug. It had. But with all the strange things currently going on in the castle and having recently met a dead boy/ghost, he certainly felt less troubled by it all than he would have six months ago.

He passed across the red book and Alice turned her attention to that. Examining the worn cover, she ran her fingers over the metal corners before opening it. "So you've read all of this from start to finish?"

Hamish blushed. "Well, no, not completely. I've read a good few pages though."

He hadn't actually looked at it since he had first taken it from the library. "It's only really people – lots of Montgomerys."

"Ah hah!" interrupted Alice, who had already began leafing through the book. "Here's an old floorplan of the castle at the back. It shows the building before the south wing was added and the dungeon in a lot more detail. It seems to be divided into different parts."

Pulling out a notepad, Alice began copying it exactly. "This way, we will have our own one should we need it," she explained, which was a very good idea as the book needed to be returned to the library before Laird Montgomery noticed it was missing.

Once Alice had finished her sketch, she picked up the archive again, flicking through the pages.

"Who is this?" she asked, pointing out Struan's face. "He looks awfully like you, especially when you were younger. Hang on, is it you?"

Hamish shook his head. "That's Struan."

"It is? Wow! He really does look like you. It's kind of spooky, the resemblance." Alice studied the young boy's picture even closer.

Hamish was about to point out his own portrait to prove it wasn't him when his cousin noticed a loose thread from the inside of the back cover had become attached to her charm bracelet. Without thinking, she snapped it off.

RIIIIIIIIIIIIIIPPPPPPPPP.

"What have you done?" gulped Hamish, feeling sick with worry. "You've gone and torn the book! My dad will go nuts. That book is hundreds and hundreds of years old."

Alice flipped all the pages forward and saw the red fabric on the inside of the back cover was indeed coming away. "Oh! I'm so sorry, Hamish. Look, I'm sure I can do something to fix it," she said, trying to smooth it down to no avail. "Hang on, what's that stuffed behind it?"

The loose piece of fabric appeared to be concealing something. Carefully, Alice pulled the rest away.

Hidden behind was a little compartment and sandwiched inside was a piece of brown paper. Unsure of how fragile it was, Alice lifted up the book and gently shook it, allowing the paper to fall out of its own accord rather than risk tearing it by prising it out with her fingers.

With the note now free and lying on the bedcover, the cousins agreed to read it together.

An auld witch

Once said,

The Montgomery Claymore

Would turn to lead

Unless,

Tears are shed

For every man dead

If not all,

Then one should fall,

From the blood of whom

Bled those dry

Only then,

Shall the past be forgiven

Only then,

Will the future be rewritten

"What does it all mean?" said Alice, baffled by the fifteen-line verse.

For Hamish, a small part of the puzzle had just slotted into place, however. "It has to be the curse!"

He immediately began reeling off the story from Ranald's little pocketbook.

"So the curse must be... Whenever anyone holds it, it turns to lead?" Alice concluded as she ran through the poem again.

"But why lead?"

Alice thought for a minute. "You said Angus didn't want the claymore to be used in battle again? Well, nobody would be able to lift and fight with a sword if it turned to lead. Not even someone as strong as Earl Angus himself."

"YOU'RE RIGHT!" said Hamish struggling to keep his voice down as they found themselves that bit closer to deciphering the mystery that surrounded the lost claymore. "That's probably why the burglars weren't able to carry it very far. What do you think the rest means? The bit about the tears and the past being forgiven and rewritten?"

Alice sat, reading the words again to herself. "I really don't know. But it's got to contain some more clues."

They sat thinking for some time.

When no inspiration came, Alice did what anyone does when they want to know more about something – she Googled it.

"Where did you get that?" Hamish looked enviously on as his cousin produced a mobile phone from the pocket of her jeans.

"It's my mum's. She just got a new contract and gave me this one to use if I need to make a phone call. It still has the Internet. She forgot to cancel it."

"And you've got a signal here?"

"Yep!"

The reception around the castle was notoriously awful. The only way his father could ever make or receive mobile calls in his study was if he stood on one leg on a chair with his chin pressed against the wall whilst flapping his left arm up and down like a duck. And only then would he pick up one measly bar of reception.

Being on the north side of the castle, several feet up a turret was helping the network coverage.

Alice used her finger to type *Montgomery Claymore* and *Drumtipperty Castle curse* into the screen.

At first, their search only brought up the little information they already knew. But as they scrolled further down the results, they found a website called *Auld Crimes Nae Solved.* Their click led them to a home page that featured a cartoon policeman angrily waving his truncheon over his head.

In no real order appeared a list of crimes that happened in Scotland over the eighteenth, nineteenth and twentieth centuries.

According to the short paragraph on Drumtipperty, the police believed a man called Gordon Abernathy masterminded the whole plot. He was arrested, along with two accomplices, outside Crathword on the night of the burglary.

Unable to provide the officer with a valid explanation as to why they were trudging along the road at 3.50 a.m., covered in mud, the men's pockets were turned out. Hidden in the lining of Gordon's jacket was a small scrap of paper with six arrows and a single cross printed on it in ink. The police were convinced it was a secret code – one they were unable to crack.

The children spent another thirty minutes searching online but found nothing more.

"Let's take another look at the archive," suggested Alice. She began to study the map of the dungeon again, turning it over. "Look, there's a log on the back."

There were three names in total, listed one after the other.

James Robertson – imprisoned for stealing vegetables from the estate – spared death, released twelve months later.

Malcolm Campbell – imprisoned for trespassing – served three weeks.

William Abernathy – imprisoned for attempted theft of a prized, blue bird – imprisoned for six years/missing/perished/presumed dead/possibly eaten by rats.

"YIKES! Eaten by rats! Can you imagine how horrible that would be?!" Hamish remarked. Thinking about the banging from the dungeon that he heard on a nightly basis, he felt a shiver run down his spine.

It was then – just seconds later – that the realisation hit both children, so hard, they almost fell off the bed.

20.

A Bit of Good News

"A blue bird! It's Lady Foo Foo Archer! That's what Mr Guillemot's BB101 said happened. Struan brought her back as a clue!" cried Hamish.

"And what about the name – William

Abernathy?" squealed Alice, her own excitement building. "It's the SAME SURNAME as one of the claymore thieves. That's way too much of a coincidence, don't you think? That one of the castle's former prisoners had the exact same last name as one of the men who tried to steal the claymore all those years later. They've got to be related, right?"

Not waiting for a reply, Alice punched the two names into the phone.

"I'm going to check the two names out on the Family Finder app. It pulls up ancestral links from hundreds of years ago."

Hamish made a mental note to tell the Laird about the app before his next birthday portrait.

On the phone's screen, an old style clock popped up. The dial rapidly spun anti-clockwise for about a minute. Numbers and dates poured out of it before a green tree began to form with names and pictures shooting off from the virtual branches.

"Look!" Alice pointed out the names on an Abernathy family history chart. "They are related! There's a couple of hundred years between them, but they are related."

Two pictures of the men appeared. Gordon looked darker, and William looked skinnier, but both had the same hooked nose and unpleasant beady eyes.

"That woman, Mrs Burwick," said Hamish pointing to a lady with a thick neck and a similarly glowering expression. "The one above and to the left of Gordon...that name sounds familiar."

"Does it?" said Alice, studying the small paragraph alongside. "The chart shows her as Gordon's great aunt."

DING, DING, DING.

Hamish's thoughts were interrupted when the

little brass bell for dinner rang out. It had been routed all the way up from the kitchen to the left corner of his bedroom. This was to save Mrs Cook from roaring "C'MN' GIT' YER' SUPPER!" It also meant that there was no excuse to be late for meals. Or indeed, to try and avoid them altogether.

"I'VE GOT IT!" said Hamish triumphantly, now remembering the name thanks to Mrs Cook and her bell ringing. "Struan told me Mrs Burwick was Drumtipperty's cook when the robbery happened! He didn't eat the pheasant stew that she made than night. Everyone else did, and they didn't wake up until almost lunchtime the next day."

"So she was in on it then, too! She must have drugged them all," Alice gasped. "The police couldn't have made the connection because of the different surnames!"

DING, DING, DING, DING, DING, DING.

The bell rang out a second time, this time for twice as long – a sure sign of Mrs Cook's growing anger.

"Come on, we'd better get going!"

Alice placed the poem in the middle of her blue notebook alongside her map and bundled the mobile away in her pocket before all three of them hurried down the castle stairs.

Tonight was lasagne. But, of course, it wasn't regular lasagne with mince, cheese sauce, and pasta. Mrs Cook had decided to do something a bit more creative, using a selection of store cupboard ingredients that were nearing or already past their sell-by date. This included a tin of baked beans, some tinned mackerel, and red lentils, all sandwiched between pasta sheets and topped with some dried-out cheddar cheese.

"Very inventive, Mrs Cook," the Laird remarked as he pushed the red mush around his plate without actually taking a bite.

"Ye ken me, Laird Montgomery. I dinnae' like fir' thangs to gan' tae waste, better it gits' used somewhere! Wait and see wit hae fir yer puddin!"

Despite not being able to eat his dinner and most likely dessert, Laird Montgomery remained in a good mood.

"I've had some fantastic news today," he said. A grin stretched over his entire face.

Hamish and Alice stopped moving their food around their own plates and looked up to listen.

"A couple from America, or should I say, their representatives, contacted me about hosting their wedding here."

Laird Montgomery said the word representatives in an Americanised voice, like the ones on TV.

"They're from LA. You know, where that big HOLLYWOOD sign is. They just *luuuuurve* little auld Scotland! He's a movie director, and she's a

Hollywood actress."

"And they want to get married here?" asked Hamish and Alice at exactly the same time. Precisely, who would want to get married at Drumtipperty Castle given its current state of disrepair seemed an obvious question.

"Yes, married here! Married on the Grand Lawn that is – in a marquee. They were meant to be getting married at Strobert Castle up in the Scottish Highlands. But two days ago there was a huge fire that destroyed half of the castle. They don't want anything burnt-looking in the photos. Apparently, no other castle in Scotland can accommodate them at such short notice. They are paying us £28,000!" the Laird squeaked, unable to contain his excitement. "For the inconvenience of it all."

"Can we have a wedding here?" asked Hamish, unsure what this would entail.

"Well, I don't see why not," said his father, picking up a forkful of food and putting it straight back down again. "I told them I would do a spot of landscaping and arrange a few bits and pieces from our side… The loos, the fireworks, and what not, but really how hard can that be? You know, I wouldn't be surprised if *HELLO!* shows up to cover it! Can you imagine, Drumtipperty Castle in *HELLO!* magazine! This may well be the start of a multi-million pound wedding business for us!"

Hamish could almost see the pound signs shining in his father's eyes.

21.

A Castle Wedding

Cherry Richardson was the most beautiful woman Hamish had ever seen. With golden coloured skin and long, honey-blonde hair, the Hollywood actress conveniently looked like a female Oscar.

In comparison, her fiancé and future husband Rupert Sugby was very short and very pale and looked like a weasel or a rat. *Yes, there was definitely something very weaselly or ratty about him*, thought Hamish as he passed his father's study, which Rupert had taken over as his own. A cardboard cut out of a star with the initials RS was now stuck to the door.

All morning the director had been barking orders into his mobile phone. "I'm telling you, I want it done. NOW, YOU HEAR ME? OR YOUR LAZY BACKSIDE WILL BE FIRED!"

Originally from Stoke in England, Rupert had directed and produced a very famous British movie called *Guts.* After that, he moved to LA in America, where he met Cherry on his sequel *Guts II*.

What on earth did she see in him? Hamish wondered as he watched Rupert scream into the phone so viciously that he looked like he was trying to eat it.

The director had decided to adopt full Scottish

attire for the occasion and was wearing a green tartan kilt. To begin with, the kilt had been far too long for him, so it was altered. Now it was much too short. It looked like a tartan mini-skirt and unflatteringly showed off Rupert's pale, skinny legs, all the way up to his even skinnier thighs.

"I want diamonds and lots of them!" he shouted as he marched back and forth. "Nothing, I repeat NOTHING, is too good for my little angel face. So go and get them NOW! OR I AM FIRING YOUR LAZY BACKSIDE!"

It was the morning of the wedding, and the castle was a hive of unusual levels of activity. There were more people than Hamish had probably seen in the rest of the year combined, all jostling around at great speed with clipboards and earpieces.

Outside, horns were being blasted. A long stream of wedding suppliers in cars and vans were queuing impatiently to get into the grounds. A gigantic black lorry parked just outside the castle was making it impossible for anyone to get in or out.

"Ooooooh, what's that smell?" asked Alice, pulling the neck of her top up to cover her mouth and nose but finding it wouldn't stretch far enough. Alice had come to join Hamish on the lawn in the hope of getting away from all of the commotion happening inside. An argument about where a pedestal of flowers should be placed had resulted in the mother of the bride tipping a glass of champagne over the mother of the groom's head.

"It's the loos." Hamish pointed towards the grey plastic toilet blocks that were being hoisted off the lorry.

Trying to get hold of outdoor toilets at such short notice had proved a problem. The portaloos had come directly from the *Up Yer Kilt* music festival in Inverness – uncleaned. An unpleasant smell of poo and wee filled the air, which wasn't helped by the easterly wind direction.

Laird Montgomery was, however, oblivious to the reek that was currently wafting around. Suffering from the first of the season's hay fever, a large wad of cotton wool was wedged up either nostril, which unbeknown to him, was very effective at blocking out the roaming stench.

Probably a good thing, thought Hamish, who was doing his utmost to stop himself gagging. His father was already in panic mode. If he knew there was a pungent smell of human waste going round, it would likely finish him off.

"Have the Highland coos arrived yet?" the Laird shouted across the lawn. He did this while consulting both watches multiple times despite the gold one remaining water-logged from the hose incident. The hands on the dial hadn't moved forward since.

Hamish gave the thumbs down.

The Highland cows or coos had been his suggestion. Much to his father's displeasure.

"Highland cows! You told her we were going to get flipping Highland cows?" was the Laird's initial reaction. And his opinion hadn't changed.

Cherry, on the contrary, had fallen in love with the idea straight away. "O-M-G, aren't they adorable?" she said when Hamish first showed her a picture of the giant tan-coloured beasts. "Yes, we've gotta have them! Aren't they the cutest with their shaggy coats and long bangs? These gorgeous guys are native to Scotland, right? They will make suuuuuch cute wedding pictures!"

Rather than adopting a pair, as his son had requested, the Laird had arranged with the neighbouring farm to loan them two for the day. Hamish was to oversee the whole thing, including the collection and disposal of all cowpats.

"It was your idea to have these blasted cows. You will be cleaning up after them, too," he had been told as a metal bucket and spade was thrust into his hands.

A green Land Rover towing a trailer with the cows was among those now queuing, and having arrived almost an hour earlier, the farmer appeared to be getting angrier with every passing minute.

BEEP. BEEP, BEEP. BEEEEEEEEEEEEEEEEEP. Three short blasts followed by a very long one, which seemed to last an entire minute before the farmer would take his fist off his car horn and relieve everyone's ears for a short period of time. Then it would start all over again.

The 4x4 had not moved an inch when Hamish first caught sight of Cherry waving at him from one of the upper windows. She was getting ready for the ceremony in his father's bedroom, which overlooked the Grand Lawn and his lookout spot.

The actress kept ducking down and popping back up.

Hamish glanced over his shoulder twice to see if she was motioning at someone else, but there was no one behind. She gestured for him to come up.

He had been told that under no circumstance should he leave his post on the Grand Lawn.

"You are responsible for the cows the entire time they are on this property," Laird Montgomery had warned, "including their delivery and return – and everything in between."

Hamish looked back at the queue. The lorry had finally completed the drop-off of the portaloos and was trying to squeeze unsuccessfully past the waiting traffic. Meanwhile, the farmer was now eleventh in line and creeping forward.

Doing some quick calculations in his head, he decided that if he was super fast, he would be back on the Grand Lawn for the farmer offloading the cows.

The ten-year-old snatched a final glance behind him and ran around the other side of the castle and climbed the three sets of stone stairs to get to the Green Room.

Before he had a chance to lift his hand to knock, the door opened.

"Hamish, you came!" said Cherry, pulling him in. "Sorry, I didn't want anyone to see me in my dress before the ceremony, especially Rupert. Ya know it's bad luck for the groom to see the bride before the wedding."

No sooner than he stepped inside, Hamish tripped up. His father's room was a mess. Cherry's clothes lay in heaps all over the floor like molehills. Bottles of toiletries, chocolate wrappers, and empty Diet Coke and Red Bull tins littered the unmade bed.

"So, I just loved your thoughts on all the Scottish stuff for the wedding, and I gotta get your opinion on something," said Cherry, apparently unfazed by the untidiness that was surrounding her.

Dressed in a white gown with long lace sleeves, she held up a thin tartan sash in each hand. One was green; the other was red.

"I was gonna wear one with my dress. The green one would match Rupert's kilt, but the red, the red is just more me, ya know?"

Hamish pretended to consider his answer. "Definitely the red one," he said after a moment or two. "The Montgomery tartan – our family tartan is a sort of reddish colour and cream, too, so it makes sense to wear that one with your dress."

Cherry smiled, revealing teeth that were as white as snow. "That makes perfect sense, Hamish. The red one it is. Do you mind helping me with it? It's not the easiest thing to get on."

Her long, dark eyelashes fluttered. *Like a peacock butterfly*, he thought.

Just as he finished helping Cherry secure the sash around her waist, there was an explosive *WHOOOOOOSH BANNNNNNNNNNNNNG* outside, followed by some screams and shouts and an almighty clatter. Then a rap at the door.

"Come on in," chirped Cherry, who was now rummaging in another mountain of stuff in search of a pair of white satin shoes.

A curly-haired woman with an earpiece and clipboard appeared around the door, looking nervous.

"The coos…the cows… a firework accidentally went off when a box was moved, and it spooked them. They've gone on a bit of a rampage. In fact, they've taken out the entire marquee!"

They all rushed to the window. Outside, two

untethered, caramel-coloured cows were galloping around in circles and churning up the grass with their hooves. The lawn was beginning to look like a potato field, and the marquee was lying at the far end in a crumpled heap.

Oh no, oh no, oh no, thought Hamish, realising he had overstayed by a good five minutes. The farmer must have got fed up waiting and dropped the coos off on the lawn unattended.

Just as Hamish was beginning to imagine how furious his father would be, a very red-faced Laird Montgomery appeared in view. Sprinting after the coos, he hurdled over boxes as he gave chase with a tent peg in hand. Behind him was an even redder-faced Rupert Sugby.

"THOSE COWS ARE FIRED! YOU'RE FIRED!" Rupert screamed, his little kilt swinging from side to side as he tried to keep up. The director didn't see the marquee peg sticking out of the ground like a stump, which tripped him clean up and sent him headfirst into a mound of fresh cow poo.

"Oh, wow, well, I guess that's that," giggled Cherry as she sashayed away from the window, towards the bedroom's large gold mirror, where she began to apply a fresh coat of lipstick.

"Ya know, I didn't really want to marry that mean l'il man anyway," the actress said to her own reflection whilst rubbing her ruby red lips together. "Don't ya think he kinda looks like a weasel?"

22.

The Old Dungeon

"We don't have a choice now, do we? Now your dad isn't getting any money for the wedding. We have to search the old dungeon. We have to. It's the only way we have any chance at finding the sword and saving the castle!"

Alice was right. That was exactly what they needed to do. They had to at least try to save the castle. Every other plan of Laird Montgomery's had gone south. In other words, it had been a disaster. It was up to them and them alone.

Rupert Sugby had refused to pay a penny of the £28,000 promised. Given the smelly portaloos, rampaging cows, and flattened marquee, this wasn't entirely without good reason. But he was also threatening to sue their BACKSIDES for ruining HIS BIG DAY.

Thankfully, Cherry was still onside.

"Don'tcha worry. No one is getting sued. Y'all did me a huuuuuuuuge favour," she reassured them as she boarded a gleaming black helicopter that had come to pick her up. "I'll deal with l'il weasel-face when we get back to LA."

The helicopter took off, whipping up the remaining muddy debris and dry cowpats on the Grand Lawn. Cherry gave a final wave from the domed window. Then she was gone.

All the people who had quickly descended on Drumtipperty left at an even quicker rate. Soon it was just the Laird, Hamish, Gorse, Alice and Mrs Cook again as if the disastrous wedding weekend had never even happened.

But it had. And the future of the castle was looking uncertain. Since those awful events, Laird

Montgomery had locked himself in his study and set up an old creaky camp bed by his desk. It was so old and so uncomfortable. The springs were like daggers needling his back. He felt such a bed would encourage him to work more and sleep less.

Not only had the Laird lost all concept of time, checking neither the plastic nor the damaged gold watch, he was not eating either. At first, Hamish thought this was a clever ploy to avoid Mrs Cook's horrible food for a few days. But when he heard his father was even refusing bread and butter, he knew there was a problem.

Instead, Laird Montgomery was downing multiple cups of coffee. He was drinking the stuff like it was going out of business – at least sixteen mugs a day, in addition to twenty espresso shots, which saw him mixing up a tablespoon of instant granules with two tablespoons of hot water and throwing back the dark sludge in one go.

As you may know, a diet consisting of only

coffee is not a healthy one. Soon enough, Laird Montgomery was a jittery, sleepless wreck with pupils the size of saucers. From the window outside, he could be seen marching around his study, occasionally hitting the floor to do a dozen press-ups or breaking out into a caffeine-fueled sprint as he tried to figure out what could possibly be done to save the family castle.

As it turned out, Hamish and Alice would be his last resort. Of course, Laird Montgomery did not know that. He never would have agreed to the pair of them disappearing off down into the old dungeon alone. The steep stone staircase was treacherous, especially in the dark. Then there was what was hidden down there. He didn't want anybody to see that. Least of all Hamish.

When morning came and the Laird had slipped into a reluctant sleep, filled with bird poo, pensioners and Highland coos, the cousins filled a small rucksack for their journey.

Forgetting to pack a drink of any kind, inside was a round of Mrs Cook's bread, two small apples (to be healthy), and a family-sized Dairy Milk chocolate bar that Alice had smuggled from her own home. Along with the food, a couple of spare torches were packed as well as Hamish's penknife and a few dog biscuits for Gorse.

Anyone living in Scotland will tell you summer brings no guarantees of good weather. And today was one of those days where the bite of the wind outside was a reminder that you were north of the border, summer or no summer. As well as wearing a thick jacket, Alice had a pair of blue gloves she had found in the pockets. "Better to be prepared than cold," she said, pulling them on.

Mrs Cook had been informed they were going for a countryside walk with Gorse. The word *long* was emphasised to allow them enough time to explore the cellar and get back without being caught or considered missing.

Each wearing one of Laird Montgomery's favoured head torches, the children lowered themselves down through the floor hatch into absolute darkness and closed the lid behind them with a dull *THUD*. First Hamish, then Alice. The ten-year-old boy insisted he lead the way, which caused some argument to begin with. Being both eleven months older and taller, Alice suggested she go first, but the younger cousin refused point blank on the principle that it was his castle or at least it would be one day. If they didn't end up losing it.

In the end, it was Gorse who led the way, bounding down the dark, narrow stairwell with far greater speed than either of them could muster on such steep steps. Despite his size, the deerhound was surprisingly nimble on his feet, and it wasn't long before he had disappeared off down the stone stairs and out of sight.

Hamish felt less sure of himself. He followed the steps with caution, counting each one in his head so he could remember how many there would be to climb on the way back up. With just the torchlight to guide them, all they could do was look ahead. Turn around and you risked a fall. One misplaced foot and you would find yourself with some painful injuries.

Hamish imagined if Struan were here, he would probably be doing little leap frogs, handstands, and cartwheels down the steps. But Struan was dead, so he didn't need to worry about falling and breaking a leg quite like they did.

As they continued to tramp deep underneath the castle, the temperature began to shift. While Hamish had always considered his bedroom the coldest place in the castle, the dungeon was a good few degrees below that. It was a sort of dank cold that seeped under your skin and squeezed your lungs.

"How much further?" called out Alice, but Hamish didn't know to answer.

One foot, then the next. Left, then right. Over and over again, they pushed on until they finally reached the bottom. Hamish pulled the extra two torches free from the rucksack and handed one to Alice.

"This one isn't working," she said, clicking the button on and off. "Did you check the batteries?"

"We'll just have to use this one," replied Hamish, who clearly hadn't checked the batteries. He shone a six-foot beam of light ahead of them.

The dungeon was a labyrinth of small dark grey stone rooms connected to one another with low, rounded ceilings. Huge iron hooks hung from above like a butcher's shop. What they had been used for in the past, neither of them wanted to think about.

"It smells down here," noted Alice, shifting her weight from foot to foot.

Rat wee, thought Hamish, but decided not to say this out loud in case his cousin was squeamish.

Many people were with rats. The giant black rodents had been frequent visitors to the castle over the years so Hamish had got quite used to them, and besides, Gorse was an expert at keeping them at bay.

"What's that noise?"

A hissing sound was coming from one of the dungeon's rooms.

Rats, thought Hamish again, hoping Gorse didn't have one cornered somewhere.

"Not the hissing," Alice added when he didn't answer. "The other sound – a sort of shaking, banging noise."

Hamish listened and heard a hollow rattling. Like the sound of something being locked in a tin box trying to get out.

They set off apprehensively, their feet following the noise, which only got louder.

CRASH, CRASH, BANG! BANNNNG, BANG!

It was the same sound that could be heard in

the evening, only not as loud. *Probably the reason why it couldn't be heard in the castle through the day*, thought Hamish.

As they moved further into the vault, he shone the extra torch against the walls to identify anything that stood out as unusual, but nothing did. The stone just looked grey and patchy. Some of it was chalky-looking and crumbling away; other bits glistened black as if it were wet and the walls were sweating. Dampness hung thickly in the air, reminding them that not once had the dungeon seen daylight.

The torch then lit up something on the wall, so insignificant they almost missed it. Three small lines had been scored into the stone, pointing in the direction of the banging noise.

"Is that an arrow?" asked Alice, going over to the wall to inspect it, while the *CRASH, CRASH, BANG, BANNNNG, BANG!* continued in the background.

"It does look like one…"

CRASH, CRASH, BANG, BANNNNG, BANG!

Two walls down, the marking was confirmed when they discovered another, followed by a third.

"Alice, remember arrows were on the burglar's piece of paper."

"Yes, has to be another non-coincidence!"

They carried on through the dungeon, which felt like an underground cave. Each stone room appeared to be the same as the last, and all were empty. The antiques had since moved upstairs for the now cancelled castle tours. Laird Montgomery had yet to move them all back down again

CRASH, CRASH, BANG, BANNNNG, BANG!

The noise was growing in volume, suggesting they were nearing the source.

CRASH, CRASH, BANG, BANNNNG, BANG!

CRASH, CRASH, BANG, BANNNNG, BANG!

Whatever it was, it wasn't more than five feet away from them.

CRASH, CRASH, BANG, BANNNNG, BANG!

CRASH, CRASH, BANG, BANNNNG, BANG!

CRASH, CRASH, BANG, BANNNNG, BANG!

With shaking hands, Hamish stuck the torch out.

23.

A Shocking Discovery

The yellow light first lit up another arrow etched into the wall. Then Gorse, who unconcerned by all the banging had his jaws locked around an old rotting plank. Shreds of wood lay around him.

To the dog's right was a huge, rusty orange piece of metal about eight-feet tall. The contraption was covered in bolts, taps, handles, and pipes. Some sort of temperature gauge was attached to the side. It was rattling so loudly, the base was lifting off the ground and thrashing against the floor. Steam was pouring out of it, too.

CRASH, CRASH, BANG, BANNNNG, BANG!

"It's the old boiler," Hamish declared with relief. "My dad said there was one down here, and it was a noisy thing!"

"Phew!" said Alice, releasing a long puff of her own breath. "I was worried that it was the ghost of William thumping about. Really, if the sound of rats wasn't bad enough!"

"That's only four arrows, though."

"What?"

"Four arrows," repeated Hamish, "Gordon Abernathy's piece of paper had six in total."

"Oh, yeah. You're right."

Leaving the noisy boiler and its bash, bash, bashing behind them, they carried on their search. The pair had almost reached the end of the dungeon when they spotted another arrow on what appeared to be the final wall seemingly pointing nowhere. As they edged forward, they could see there was a small stone chamber hidden around the corner at the very back. The glow of their torchlight then picked up something sharp, shiny, and metal-looking.

Could it be... Surely not... Could it?

The cousins looked at one another, not daring to utter the word claymore aloud in case they somehow jinxed it. Their blood rushed with excitement. The light bounced around the cellar as they both broke out into a run.

When they turned the corner, they discovered the long piece of metal was not the sword they had hoped for, however, but rather an abandoned clothes pole. The room was full of metal racks filled with dresses and coats. A wooden dressing table sat alongside, piled high with jewellery.

It was all of Hamish's mother's things.

"Wait, what's it all doing down here?" said Alice as she ran a gloved hand along some clothes before tugging out at a long green, glittery dress from the rack and pulling it over her anorak. Keeping her sports socks on, she kicked off her trainers and slipped on a pair of black, shiny shoes that were three sizes too big.

Hamish touched a colourful printed dress he was sure he could remember his mum wearing on the beach, then a sparkly jumper that made him think of Christmas.

For a split second, he had a terrible notion. What if his father had kept his mother prisoner in the cellar for all these years? Maybe like the burglars before her, she escaped and was too scared to come back and live with them again.

"You don't think... You don't think... He... Would've..."

"Hamish, no!" Alice said, not letting him finish his sentence. "Your dad hasn't been keeping your mum hidden away down here. I know he's got a bit dour over the last few years, but there's no way he would do that. My mum told me he was devastated when it all happened – when she left. I think he's kept all her things because he didn't want to let them go."

"Maybe he's saving them for when she comes back," said Hamish, his voice full of hope. Neither of them spoke for a while, wondering if she ever would.

It was the older cousin who finally broke the silence. "Do you mind if I take this?" She pulled up the cuff of her jacket to reveal a small chain attached to her wrist above her own charm bracelet, inscribed *AM.* Arabella Montgomery. Unlike the rest of the jewellery stacked in the cellar, it wasn't glitzy or showy. It was just plain but all the prettier for having his mother's initials on.

Hamish agreed, slipping a bottle of perfume he found on the dresser into his own jacket pocket. This one would replace the old one, which had almost run out.

"So I guess we've found your mum's treasure or maybe even your dad's treasure, depending on how you look at it, but we have yet to find the castle's treasure – the claymore. We'd better keep searching."

"But we've looked everywhere," complained Hamish, his frustration beginning to grow.

"Let's not give up yet. Let me check the floor plan."

As Alice removed her notebook from the inside of her jacket pocket, Gorse appeared around the corner to join them.

"That's it, I'm afraid. The cellar doesn't go any further," she said, borrowing the torch from Hamish to shine it between the drawing in her notebook and the back wall. "Hey, wait a minute, do you see that?"

Above a clothes rail filled with fur jackets in various browns and blacks was another arrow, the smallest of all six. It was different from the rest in that it pointed down rather than to the side.

"The sixth and final arrow!"

Together, the cousins pushed the rack aside. The pole made a scraping noise against the stone floor like fingernails down a chalkboard.

Behind the rail were several loose bricks. Nine of them in total. Some of them came away easier than others. The final brick took the longest to remove despite not having any other blocks surrounding it. When it was pulled out and placed on the pile, they spotted that an *X* had been scratched into it. The initials *WA* were underneath.

"*WA*! It's got to be the prisoner, William Abernathy!" said Alice. "He must have carved the arrows into the walls, too. But why?"

Hamish crouched down and stared into the pit of blackness – the sort that swallowed you up whole. "*X* marks the spot," he replied as Alice knelt down next to the hole. "This is a secret escape route out of the castle."

24.

The Secret Escape Tunnel

From the little they could see, the underground tunnel looked like a large rabbit burrow. A few short planks of wood held a ceiling of soil up. If the stairs down to the cellar were worrisome, this was a million times worse.

Neither cousin volunteered to go first.

"William Abernathy must have somehow dug his way out of the dungeon and made a map." Hamish said instead.

"And Gordon Abernathy must have got his hands on William's old map, arranged the burglary, and used the tunnel to steal the sword without being seen, not knowing that the claymore was cursed and would turn to lead as they tried to carry it away," Alice added in turn.

"You know, Alice, I think it actually might be too dangerous to go down there," said the younger cousin after a long pause. "The tunnel is so old it could well collapse on us."

"Yeah, I agree. I just don't think we can risk it."

Feeling disappointed that their grand plan had amounted to nothing more than a bracelet and bottle of perfume, they were still peering into the black hole when something shot out from underneath the rack of fur jackets.

As Hamish suspected, it was a rat and a very large one at that. It raced along the dark stone floor, a long tail sweeping behind a squat, black body. Scuttling off in the direction of the boiler, the rat clocked Gorse. Both rodent and dog looked at one another, and for a brief moment neither moved. The rat then embarked on its escape route. Doubling back, it leapt over Alice's shoulder like an Olympic long jump athlete, flew through the air, and dive-bombed into the tunnel. Gorse responded by disappearing in immediately after.

"The rat touched me! Its tail touched me!" Alice shrieked, wriggling her shoulders up and down in disgust.

"Gorse has gone after that rat! Gorse! GORSE, COME BACK!" yelled Hamish, who was far more concerned for the deerhound. He began to flash the torch inside the hole, but the strobes of light lit up very little.

Several minutes passed, and the dog's wet nose still did not pop back up. After a further ten minutes of shouting, Hamish took a deep breath. "I have to go in. I can't leave Gorse down there."

Alice nodded. "I'll come with you." The tunnel looked frightening, but the prospect of staying alone in the dungeon with a bunch of rats was equally bad.

Getting on all fours, Hamish began crawling into the small dirt opening. Alice was not far behind. Even on their knees, their heads grazed the top of the mud-packed roof, knocking little bits of soil away as they went.

The tunnel didn't follow a straight line. Instead, it turned and twisted. One minute they were crawling up, and the next, down. The constant change in direction meant they couldn't see more than three metres ahead or anticipate what would come next.

They had reached another downhill slope when they first heard muffled barks coming from further along the passageway.

"BARK, BARK, BARK!"

"He's got to be close," said Hamish, trying to increase his speed a little. "Gorse we are coming! Hang on in there!"

It took another hill climb on their knees before they found the deerhound. Gorse was covered in dirt and looking very sorry for himself but unharmed. The rat was nowhere in sight, having likely scarpered along the tunnel.

"Come on Gorse, we had better head back," instructed Hamish, his dirty face now wet too, having been slobbered on by the grateful dog.

But as Alice attempted to turn round and navigate back, there was a loud *CRASSSSSSH.* Clouds of muddy air puffed up. One side of the tunnel's walls had caved in behind, blocking them from going back the way they had just come from.

"We could have been buried under that," she whispered, her voice frightened.

With that part of the tunnel impassable, they had no choice but to continue onwards in hope that it led somewhere. The little air that there was in the tunnel was now filled with dust and particles of dirt. This was what being buried alive must feel like, thought Alice.

"Come on, we have to keep going," said Hamish, starting to crawl again and encouraging Gorse, who was ahead of him, to move off again. He wished he too had worn gloves. His fingernails were crammed with dirt, and his palms were bruised from all the crawling. It wasn't just his hands either. Every bone in his body was beginning to ache, especially his back. He had to curve his spine downwards to avoid knocking the ceiling, and he was pretty sure his knees were bleeding, too.

Hamish looked back and saw from his cousin's face that she was also struggling. Alice was relying on her left arm to pull her way through and her legs to push, which made crawling along the narrow tunnel all the more difficult. Small beads of sweat were beginning to surface above the grime on her forehead.

If the passageway wasn't small enough, it seemed to get even smaller when they came to the next bend. Roots hung from the ceiling like fine hair. The three of them scrabbled on, Gorse sometimes having to push himself along on his belly because the ceiling was so low. No one spoke. Everyone was too tired. And too scared. Especially when large chunks of mud started falling from above, showering them with dirt.

"Get on your stomach like Gorse. Keep your head and your back low as you crawl," commanded the younger cousin as more soil gave way.

The tunnel then did something different. It went up and continued to do so. Up and up they crawled. There seemed to be more air circulating. The walls of mud were less dense. As they turned the next corner, the tunnel seemed a little less black, too.

Even more reassuring, they began to see two small corners of light up ahead. Hamish felt his spirits soar. They appeared to be moving towards ground level. Could they be approaching the end? He prayed so. Never in his life had he felt so exhausted. "Fair wabbit," was how Mrs Cook would describe such tiredness.

The tunnel began to get wider, and Hamish was able to squeeze past Gorse to have a proper look. The opening ahead was a bit bigger than a football and divided into two small moon shapes. Sitting diagonally across the gap was a metal pole of some sort wedged into the ground.

"I don't know if that's a water pipe or something, but it's blocking us in," panted Hamish upon reaching it. He sat himself down in the tunnel and pushed his shoulder hard against it, and then his hand, to see if it would budge. "OUCH! The thing cut me." He held up a muddy hand that was now bloody, too.

"Hamish, it's not a pipe then!" said Alice, catching her breath and taking a seat herself. "A pipe wouldn't cut you like that!"

The cousins looked at one another.

The claymore!

They had clean forgotten what they had come in search for. All they had been thinking about was trying to get out of the tunnel alive.

Hamish tried to pull at it again, grazing his hand again. "OUCH!"

"Here, use my gloves," said Alice passing them

across. But even with the gloves protecting his hands, he couldn't move the sword.

"It's no use. It's not working!" said Hamish. "It's stuck solid. The claymore must have turned to lead when it was being stolen, and the burglars weren't able to pull it out of the tunnel. Over the years the earth must have closed up around it."

He couldn't believe it. They had finally found the Montgomery Claymore. But not only could they not move it, it was trapping them inside the tunnel and leaving them with no way out. The very thing that was supposed to save the castle was threatening their lives!

25.

A Near Death Situation

Just when it seemed that all hope was lost, Alice began rummaging in her jacket pocket and produced the very thing that could save them – the mobile phone.

Hamish felt his heart thump with joy. “YES! You brought the mobile!”

“Yeah. My mum said I should always keep it on me. To be used only in emergencies.”

This, they both agreed, was an emergency. But when Alice tried calling Laird Montgomery, her mum, and then the police, the phone kept cutting out.

“There’s no signal down here!”

“Try again.”

Alice tried and tried again, but still the phone

wouldn't connect.

Hamish felt his heart plummet below his rib cage again. "Let's try later," he said, deciding not to waste the phone's battery. "We may as well shout and see if someone hears us."

They took it in turns so they wouldn't use their voices all up at once.

"HELP, HELP, HELP!"

"HELP, HELP, HELLLLLLLP, SOMEONE PLEASE HELP US!"

But no one came, not even when Gorse joined in with a chorus of barks and long howls.

"We're trapped, aren't we?" said Alice. "No one knows where we are. How will they ever find us if we are underground?"

Hamish had no clue where they were either. They could have crawled all the way to Crathword for all he knew. It certainly felt like they had.

Pushing his head out over the sword as far as he could without slicing his neck open, he could see lots of grass. Grass wasn't much of a clue, though. Grass was everywhere.

He tried again, twisting his body backwards to see if there was anything else he recognised – a landmark or something.

Out of the very corner of his eye, he spotted something. It was the giant oak tree, the one Struan had fallen from all those years ago and the one that had appeared in the painting. From that tree, he knew exactly where they were – about two miles walk north of the castle.

Phew, at least they were still on Drumtipperty's grounds, Hamish thought. But was that actually a good thing? The only people who ever ventured out this far were himself and Gorse. He suddenly felt the same amount of worried as when they were deep in the belly of the tunnel with no clear way out.

"Pass me out my penknife from the back pocket of the rucksack, please," he said having an idea, albeit a desperate one.

Alice pulled it out and handed the red knife over. Her cousin opened it up and started chiseling away at the ground where the sword entered at either end. But it was much too stony, and the small blade began to bend under the pressure until it snapped.

Furious, Hamish threw the penknife so that it bounced a few metres along the mud floor. "STUPID THING! I'm not sure we are ever going to get out of here. What are we going to do?"

"Let's keep shouting," was all that Alice could suggest. The mobile phone continued to show no sign of reception.

"HELP, HELP!"

"BARK, BARK, BARK!"

"HELP, HELP! PLEASE HELP US!"

After three long hours of shouts and pleas, no help came. In that time, Gorse had snuffled out all of the dog biscuits, the loaf of bread, and the apples from the rucksack and eaten the entire lot, cores and all. Alice rationed out some pieces of the Dairy Milk to Hamish and herself, grateful Gorse had at least left them the chocolate, given it was poisonous to him anyway.

"I'm sorry," Hamish said, biting his lip, which tasted of both mud and chocolate. "I didn't think this would happen."

"You don't need to apologise. I said we should go down to the dungeon in the first place," offered his cousin.

"Yes, but I was the one who wanted to go after Gorse."

"We couldn't leave him down there. Let's agree it's both our faults," said Alice. "We are both as stupid as one another!"

"Agreed," he said, not quite managing a smile.

The changing light suggested the afternoon was coming to a close. Hamish once again pushed his head out of the small gap over the claymore. Behind him, Gorse was snoring, unaware of the terrible situation they were in. Meanwhile Alice, who was covered in so much dirt that she looked as if she were part of the tunnel, sat quietly crying.

He began to think about his father and wondered if in his sleep-deprived haze he had noticed they were missing. Surely he and Mrs Cook would come and look for them at some point.

Feeling the bottle of perfume in his jacket, Hamish pulled it from his pocket and inhaled the sweet floral scent and felt more alone than ever. Having not cried for many months, possibly even years, for the second time in just ten days his eyes welled up. He shook his head, trying to shake off the emotion bubbling up inside but couldn't stop a single tear from escaping. It splashed on the blade below.

In that instant, the ten-year-old will always claim he saw a bright white light. Laird Montgomery would say his son was delirious from dehydration and exhaustion and on a sugar rush from the Dairy Milk.

Shielding his eyes with his hand, Hamish then saw what he thought was a white horse, galloping towards the mouth of the tunnel. Flecks of grass and mud were flying up from under the animal's pounding hooves that at times appeared as if they were trampling over orange flames and then splashing through pools of ice blue water. As the horse drew nearer, he could see there was a very old man sitting on top wearing a burgundy and cream kilt.

It was Earl Angus. Back down to earth as a ghost, Hamish was sure of it. Like Struan, the old man had come to help them. He had come for his claymore, and he had brought his horse with him.

While considering this latest resurrection, the ground above began to shake, and another sheet of mud washed over him. The tunnel appeared to be on the brink of collapse, and Hamish began to fear his own death was near. Even if the underground passage managed to hold, there seemed a real possibility that he would be trampled on, particularly as the stallion's stomping legs were now within arm's reach.

Peering out from his underground peephole, Hamish held his breath and prepared for impact. He was about to squeeze his eyes shut to block out the inevitable agony that would come with such a horrible end when he saw a large pale hand reach down. It was about the size of a spade, dotted with brown spots and striped with blueish veins. It was missing a middle finger.

The hand wrapped around the metal.

WHOOOOOOOOOOOSHHHHHHHHHHHH.

CRACCCCCCCCCCCCCCCCCCCCCCCCCK.

SHHHHHHHHHHHHHHHHHHHHHHHH.

Suddenly, the soil started crumbling away, and a gap appeared, large enough for them to clamber through. One by one, Hamish, Alice, and Gorse slowly crawled out looking like the living dead. All three fell on to the ground and stretched their bodies, making angels in the long, summer grass, simply because they had the space to do so.

Dust and dirt had found its way into every crevice of Hamish's face. Up his nose and in his ears and mouth. He began to think of the muddy stone, the oak tree, and themselves in the old painting. It was as if the story had been told before it had actually happened.

After Hamish blinked away enough dirt that he was able to regain some vision, he began to scan the grassy park. Earl Angus and his white horse were nowhere to be seen. They had disappeared into thin air as if they had never been there in the first place.

His eyes settled on the heap of dirt where the tunnel once was. It seemed to have closed up behind them. He ran back across and desperately began digging it out with his hands, raking the soil away at great speed so clumps flew through the air. As he pushed away more and more mud, a glint of metal began to show underneath the earth.

"Hamish! The claymore! How did you do it?"

Alice came over to join him, just as he freed the sword of dirt. "How did you manage to get it out of the ground?"

Before he was able to answer, his cousin threw her arm around him, and in doing so, her notebook slipped from her jacket pocket and on to the ground.

"You've saved us and the castle!" she said as she squeezed him tightly. Next, she ran over to Gorse to give him a big hug, too. "Silly, silly rat-catcher!" she cooed.

With dirty hands, Hamish picked up the blue book, pulling out the loose piece of paper they had read previously in his bedroom. Leaving muddy thumbprints stamped on its corners, he began to reread the poem.

An auld witch

Once said,

The Montgomery Claymore

Would turn to lead

Unless,

Tears are shed

For every man dead

If not all,

Then one should fall,

From the blood of whom

Bled those dry

Only then,

Shall the past be forgiven

Only then,

Will the future be rewritten

The words finally made sense. He was the blood of Earl Angus – he was a descendant. His tear had fallen on to the sword.

What had Struan said? "Sometimes there's strength in weakness."

He couldn't believe it! A single tear had ended the claymore's curse!

As he marvelled at this miracle, the oak leaves above rustled loudly in the evening's breeze, and Hamish wondered if the ghost boy was sitting up on one of the branches, watching and celebrating, too.

26.

Docked

It was blowing what Scottish people call a hoolie when Mrs Montgomery clambered off the boat at Balantyne Harbour. Winter at sea – the North Sea, felt like a physical assault.

The first she experienced five years ago had been the worst. Giant waves rose up like sea monsters, inhaling their fishing boat and spitting it out. They were pulled this way and that, up and down, side to side, and almost under. The roar of the water had been deafening. Like being punched in the ear over and over again.

Even on the days the weather was gentler, the waves still churned. And the wind was always there, too, torpedoing the vomit back into her face, quicker than it could leave her pretty, heart-shaped mouth.

This was not how things were supposed to turn out. She had imagined life at sea would be an adventure, glamorous even—a gleaming white yacht, movie-star sunglasses, and a fruity cocktail—all while sailing warm, turquoise oceans.

Instead, she found herself onboard an old fishing trawler, ploughing through the most torrid of water, black like the night's sky, and deadly, should you take a tumble over the side. For no man would come to your aid. They were superstitious like that. One way or another, the sea gods would have their sacrifice. "The sea maun hae it's nummer," the crew warned with narrowed eyes. If a life was saved, the rescuer's would be taken in its place.

Women had long been considered a bad omen at sea, and indeed her own presence onboard was considered 'ill-luckit'. So she was ignored, and when they weren't ignoring her, they spoke in a language she couldn't much understand or said things that turned her cheeks crimson to repeat.

"Like a fish out of water," she would murmur as she watched the weatherworn men heave in their swollen nets, emptying a landslide of silver fish on to the wet deck to squirm in their thousands.

Mrs Montgomery was responsible for recording the boat's catches and landings and the conditions at sea. Her handwriting was something she once took pride in. It had always been very neat and tidy. Yet onboard the boat, it resembled more of a scrawl. And on the days that were very stormy, the conditions in the logbooks were documented not by ink but by splotches of sick.

The weather at sea was not something Mrs Montgomery needed to trouble herself with today, however. That very morning, the trawler had chugged into the blustery harbour and docked beside other bobbing boats in blues and whites.

Making her way along the pier and up through the cobbled stone streets, her black coat flew behind her like a cape. She went first to Smyth's, the ice-cream parlour, for a three-scoop cone with hot fudge sauce, whipped cream and sprinkles. She had been dreaming about that for a long time. Next, she headed across to the newsagent. The door made a loud *DING* as she walked in, her sharp heels tapped the white floor tiles, which reeked of fresh bleach. *Better than mackerel, haddock or whiting*, she thought.

Mrs Montgomery was sick to the gills of fish and baked beans, baked beans and fish. Then more fish and baked beans. Then just fish when their cupboards had run dry a week earlier.

Chocolate, she really wanted some chocolate. Now what should she have? Not a Twix or a Mars. What else did they have? She certainly didn't want a Bounty.

She pushed a Double-Decker on to the counter with a pound coin. *A magazine*, she thought, I'll get one of those, too. A lot of reading was done at sea. With a limited TV and WIFI signal, there really wasn't much else to do. Too much thinking time at sea wasn't good for the mind either. Not hers, anyway.

She scanned the small line-up and was about to reach for her usual favourite from the rack, *Fash Quines,* when she spotted the latest issue of

HELLO! to its left. On the cover it said, "Inside: Take a sneak peek at Drumtipperty Castle – one of Scotland's oldest castles rediscovers its fortunes thanks to an ancient sword."

Mrs Montgomery plucked out a copy and began to read.

27.

A Letter from the North Sea

The first flurries of snow were falling. Some were beginning to cling to the diamond-shaped windowpanes of Drumtipperty Castle's kitchen, where Laird Montgomery and Hamish sat eating hot porridge with treacle for breakfast.

The electricity had been restored, and a new boiler had replaced the old one, meaning that the castle was once again warm – or as warm as an old castle could be – which wasn't very warm at all.

Despite the dining room now being an (almost) comfortable temperature to sit, the pair chose to continue eating their meals in the kitchen.

Since the discovery of the Montgomery Claymore, life had changed at Drumtipperty.

It began with a visit from a reporter called Andrew Groves. The young man appeared unannounced one Thursday afternoon, an Adam's apple protruding from a long thin neck like he had swallowed a conker. He came brandishing a notepad and a laminated *Crathword Chronicle* business card that he flashed at the door as if it were a police officer's badge.

The Laird, who was much better at dealing with members of the public these days, welcomed the reporter in with a pat on the shoulder. When it was discovered Andrew's father had also gone to Graceford, he provided a friendly yet vigorous backslap, too.

"Robert Groves! Bob Groves! Bobby Groves. Ah, Grovey, that's what we used to call him. He was pretty good at rugby, you know! Broke his nose three times, though."

Laird Montgomery had not escaped his own years of playing the sport, and his ears stuck out at slightly odd angles from his head. "So you want to know all about the Montgomery Claymore? Well, it was down to Hamish really. He was the hero who found it."

The Laird led the reporter through into the castle's reception. "Yes, he was the boy who saved this castle! Hamish and his cousin Alice wrapped their jackets around the sword and balanced it on good old Gorse's back – built like a carthorse that dog is! Together, they carried it back for two miles."

"What did you say when you saw it? Were you shocked?" asked Andrew, scribbling furiously on his notepad.

"Was I shocked? Was I shocked?" said the Laird. "My eyes almost popped out of my head! But I had never seen the original sword myself."

To begin with, he had questioned if it was in fact the real Montgomery Claymore, but he didn't tell Andrew that.

The Montgomery Claymore was black. That's what he had been told all those years ago, and everything he had read had suggested the same. But the sword Hamish and Alice had returned with was a grubby silver.

The first thing he did when the two exhausted, mud-covered children and dog arrived back at the castle late in the evening was to hug them all very tightly. The second thing was to tell them how worried he and Mrs Cook had been. The third and final thing was to lead the children into the drawing room. There he showed them the painting of Angus Montgomery with his claymore, just as his grandfather had done before him.

"I'm afraid this can't be the Montgomery Claymore. It's not the same colour."

While pointing out the large black sword clutched in Angus's huge hand, Laird Montgomery noticed a spattering of fresh bird droppings on the canvas.

The week before, he and the blasted Lady Foo Foo Archer had come to a sort of truce, although he wasn't sure she completely understood. But under the agreement he had pitched, she was to let him come and go as he pleased without attack, and he would reintroduce the twice daily bucket of bread.

As part of the arrangement, the bird was limited to doing her business on a blue plastic sheet, laid out on the floor, and for the most part, she obliged. It had taken a bit of practice, but Lady

Foo Foo Archer had begun to get the hang of it.

"Idiot bird," the Laird moaned. "She's missed that darn plastic sheet. Really, how hard is it to take aim on to that? We are far bigger than her and manage to do use a toilet, which is far smaller than that blasted blue sheet!"

Spitting on a white handkerchief that he kept in his trouser pocket, he reached up and began to rub the mark on the painting. As he moved the cloth over the canvas, it quickly became black.

At first, the Laird thought he might have somehow damaged the artwork, but it was only that bit with the blade where the black colour was lifting from, nowhere else. As he kept rubbing, more and more black came away.

What was underneath almost made his heart stop. There was still a sword there but a silver one – identical to the one Hamish, Alice, and Gorse had just returned with.

"IT'S THE SAME SWORD!" shouted

Hamish, immediately noticing the changing colour. "LOOK! It's exactly the same one as we've found!"

Laird Montgomery stood very still. He looked like he may faint. "I don't understand. Was the painting dirty? Was it dirt just making the claymore black?"

Hamish and Alice looked at each other, wondering the same. Or had breaking the witch's curse somehow changed it? After all, the painting had reverted back to its original state with Earl Angus and the white horse. They were no longer in it. The oak tree had also disappeared as had Lady Foo Foo Archer's outline in it.

For that matter, where was the blue bird? Hamish thought, noticing the bucket of bread underneath the fireplace was untouched. Her not scoffing her food in two minutes flat was highly unusual.

It took several more minutes of the Laird

looking between the painting and the claymore and back again before finally conceding, "It was indeed the same sword."

Soon, he and the two children were jumping like they were on invisible trampolines. "IT'S THE SAME SWORD!" they shouted. "IT'S THE SAME SWORD!"

Not one to be left out, Gorse leapt around, too, shaking his coat and sending bits of mud scattering across the floor.

It was this exact spot, where it was still a bit crunchy underfoot, that the Laird began to retell the events of that night to Andrew in a drawing room, which was now at least free of bird poo.

No one was quite sure how, or precisely when, Lady Foo Foo Archer left. There was no obvious exit route. The drawing room windows remained shut, and the door locked. Her departure had, however, coincided with the discovery of the claymore.

According to Mr Guillemot and his tracking device, the blue pheasant was flying over the Indian Ocean, possibly in transit to China.

"She has an internal compass, a built-in homing system that must be guiding her back to her natural habitat," he had explained to Hamish and the Laird when he appeared at the castle not more than an hour ahead of Andrew, having finally got his old blue car fixed.

Of course, the bird's inexplicable appearance and disappearance all added to the reporter's story and the following week, "SILVER SWORD SAVES 874-YEAR-OLD CASTLE" *by Andrew Groves* headlined the *Crathword Chronicle.* Inside the paper, a shorter piece read "Mysterious Extinct Blue Bird Back from the Dead Journeys Across World". A small picture of Mr Guillemot and his tracking device was also included.

Within twenty-four hours of the newspaper articles being published, a helicopter was flying over Drumtipperty Castle like a giant insect. Four news crews arrived, each barreling up the driveway in minivans with BBC News, ITV, Sky, and Channel 4 splashed across their metal panelling.

When Laird Montgomery opened the door, he was greeted with flashes of cameras and shouts of questions.

"Mr Montgomery, has the real Montgomery Claymore been found?"

"Can we see the sword?"

"Are you planning on selling it on eBay?"

"Laird Montgomery, does the sword have magical powers?"

"Is the claymore cursed?"

"What do you plan to do with the sword?"

"Some people are saying it's a fake. What do you say to them?"

"Is it true you have been breeding a once extinct blue bird by the name of Lady Foo Foo Archer?"

The old Laird Montgomery would have slammed the castle door on the rabble and retired to his study with a cup of watery tea. But the new Laird Montgomery offered a wide smile. No longer did he have that sinking feeling in his belly. The sword had given him hope.

"Right, ladies and chaps, it is cold outside," he said with a quick check of his gold watch that now told the time reliably. Andrew Grove's exclusive on Drumtipperty had landed the reporter a job with *The Daily Telegraph* in London, a promotion that the boy's father, Robert Groves, was most grateful for and the broken watch had been fixed the previous day as a thank you.

"Who wants a cup of coffee and some cake?" continued the Laird, rubbing his hands together to warm them up. "I believe Mrs Cook has just made a fresh batch of banana and bacon breakfast muffins. Then we can get started. There's a lot for us to cover. I'm not sure that you know, but

Drumtipperty Castle and the history of the Montgomerys date back 874 years, 875 come the New Year."

Since that day, happily referred to as the press invasion, there had been a series of well-paying TV and magazine interviews. The BBC had also been in contact about filming an episode of the *Antiques Roadshow* in the spring.

"Things are definitely on the up," remarked Laird Montgomery while he and Hamish finished the remaining porridge and discussed the castle's latest coverage in *HELLO!* magazine on pages four, five and seven.

To begin with, the *TAP, TAP* noise at the kitchen window was masked by the scrapes of spoons against bowls as they cleaned them of porridge. It was only once their cutlery had quietened that they noticed a large seagull was sitting behind the patchwork of glass, peering in.

"What is that idiot bird doing here and so far

from the sea?" said Laird Montgomery, who remained suspicious of anything with wings and a digestive system.

Its long yellow beak continued to rap at one of the panes.

Hamish reached up and pulled the handle of the narrow window open, allowing the bird to stroll through. Pausing on the stone ledge inside, it ruffled its feathers in the cold gasps of air.

"Look, there's a note attached to its foot!" pointed the ten-year-old. Obligingly, the seagull stuck one long orange leg out for the small scroll of paper to be untied.

"It's addressed to you, Dad. The postmark says it's from the North Sea."

As Laird Montgomery took the note from his son and opened it, the bird hopped back out of the window. Unfolding its giant wings, it flew off in the direction it had come.

"What is it, Dad?"

The Laird's face had turned the same white as the paper. Feathery snow continued to blow through the open window, coating the shoulder of his dressing gown like dandruff.

"It's from… It's from your mother, Hamish. She read about the sword. She wants to come to Drumtipperty. She wants to come and see us."

To be continued…